THERE GOES DEATH

There Goes Death

A Patrick Dawlish Mystery

John Creasey *writing as* **Gordon Ashe**

ISBN: 978-1-5040-9876-2

This edition published in 2025 by Open Road Integrated Media, Inc.
180 Maiden Lane
New York, NY 10038
www.openroadmedia.com

THERE GOES DEATH

CHAPTER ONE

NOT SAFE TO KNOW

'I don't mind admitting,' said Robbie Graham, 'that I've got the wind up. I can stand some things, but—confound it, Pat, what would you feel like if you'd been pushed off a platform in front of a train, shoved under a bus, and then sniped at while cycling along a country lane?'

Graham's chubby face held an expression suggesting that being sniped at in a country lane was the last straw. Anywhere else, he might have said, it would have been understandable. He looked about him, spotted a steward, and hailed him.

'What will you have?' he demanded of Dawlish.

'Beer, thanks,' said Dawlish, waking up.

Robbie ordered beer, shrugging good-humouredly at his story's flat reception.

'What are you doing now?' he asked.

'I'm at Whitehall.'

'Good Lord!' exclaimed Robbie, his eyes becoming round saucers of commiseration. 'No wonder you look peeved. I mean,' he went on hastily, 'no chance of doing anything or going anywhere. You used to be a one for getting around, too.' He leapt to his feet. 'Well, cheerio, old boy. I'll be seeing you one of these days.'

He walked swiftly across the large, high-ceilinged room. About him there was a drone of conversation from the depths of thirty or so armchairs.

Robbie cut through them unnoticing and unhearing.

He had kept his story to himself for several days, but when he had seen Dawlish he had felt that at last he had found a man who would not scoff. The result had been rather less than he had anticipated.

Robbie pushed open the swing doors; one man followed him.

The man had been sitting within earshot of the conversation between Robbie and Dawlish, hidden in a deep armchair. At the moment of Robbie's departure, he had put aside an evening paper, stood up, stretched, then sauntered across the room. He followed Robbie as far as the great central hall, and was waiting on the steps when Robbie came from the cloak-room with his hat, stick, and gloves. Robbie glanced at, and away from him, then stepped into the Mall, making for St. James's Park.

It was a pleasant Autumn evening, and there were a fair amount of people about. A small group of them stood near the pond, watching the water-fowl.

Robbie walked past, deciding to take a short-cut to Whitehall, and the grey-haired but youthful-looking man followed at a good pace.

'Dawlish was darned disappointing,' thought Robbie, more than a little bitterly. 'I suppose it does seem a tall story, but at least he might have pretended to believe me.' He looked both ways before stepping into the road, crossed Whitehall, and approached Westminster Bridge. He walked slowly to the parapet and looked over, while the grey-haired man approached and then stood near him.

Robbie stared, unseeing, down at the water.

'It's a grand sight, isn't it?' said the grey-haired man.

'Er,' said Robbie, in no mood for casual conversation.

'A bit different from what it used to be,' continued the other. 'Good Lord, look at that swan! I haven't seen a swan so far down the river for years!' He craned his neck over the bridge, and in spite of himself Robbie followed his example. The swan, it seemed, was disappearing under one of the arches. The grey-haired man gripped Robbie's arm in his excitement; and then Robbie gasped, for he felt a sharp pain in his arm.

He half turned, but found himself unable to control his movements. He saw a pair of cold grey eyes and felt himself propelled towards the parapet.

Vaguely, he thought: 'Dawlish, well I'm damned!'

Dawlish, in turn, was gripping the elbow of the grey-haired man.

The latter let Robbie go. Inert, barely conscious, the youngster slumped down to the pavement.

'What the devil are you doing?' snarled the grey-haired man to Dawlish. 'Let me go!'

'Not for a long, long time,' said Dawlish softly. 'Open your hand, little man.' He twisted the man's right wrist, and from it something which glittered in the evening sun dropped to the ground and broke. A policeman looked at them inquisitively.

'That's better,' said Dawlish. 'Now you can take your choice. Pretend to be with me and liking it, or go with the oncoming bobby who's hurrying towards us. Suit yourself.'

The grey head nodded sulkily.

'You see,' said Dawlish in a louder voice, 'we shouldn't have let Robbie come out; he's just not up to it.' He turned to the constable. 'Hallo,' he greeted affably. 'You might call us a cab, Constable, our friend has been taken ill.'

'Those confounded doctors!' the grey-haired man mumbled. 'They said he was well enough to get about.'

'You can't tell with cases of shock,' said Dawlish gravely. 'Would you mind, Constable?'

The constable, after a moment's indecision, beckoned a taxi, then turned to Dawlish: 'Isn't it—er—Captain Dawlish?'

'That's right,' admitted Dawlish. 'Don't tell me I'm recognised as quickly as that.'

'I don't often forget a face, sir,' said the constable complacently. Together they helped Robbie into the cab, while the grey-haired man stood by.

Dawlish imagined him to be deliberating the chances of making a breakaway, and deciding against it.

'Thanks,' said Dawlish as Robbie was stowed in a corner seat. 'Give my regards to Superintendent Trivett when you see him.'

He rested a hand on the grey-head's arm and urged him into the cab. 'Brook Street,' he said clearly. 'Number 31c.'

He clambered in, sitting on one of the tip-up seats, then, waiting until the cabby had reached Whitehall, slid open the glass partition. 'Make that 88g Jermyn Street, will you?'

'Right, sir.'

That done, Dawlish settled back without speaking. Silence was a powerful weapon in a war of nerves and he was starting one with the grey-haired man. He saw, with satisfaction, the apprehension in the other's eyes. The cab turned into Jermyn Street, and stopped outside Number 88g.

Dawlish said quietly:

'Get out and ring the bell of Flat 3.'

The man scrambled past him. Dawlish followed, too closely for escape. There was a short pause before a tall, slim girl opened the door. She said in a half-laughing, half-chiding voice:

'Pat, you idiot, why did you ring?'

'Is Ted upstairs?'

'No, he's gone out for half an hour.'

'That's a pity. Darling, hop along the road and ask Fraser to look in right away, will you?'

The girl looked at him with quick understanding, then nodded and ran along Jermyn Street.

Dawlish turned to his prisoner. 'We're going to carry Graham up to the flat, and if you try any tricks I'm going to break your neck.'

The man's breathing was heavy and laboured as they carried Robbie up two flights of stairs. Reaching a small landing where one door was ajar, Dawlish edged it wider open with his elbow. They went through without difficulty, and Dawlish led the way to a small bedroom. He laid Robbie on the bed, then straightened up.

The grey-haired man said tensely:

'What are you going to do?'

'You'll see,' said Dawlish. 'We're going into the other room.'

Ostentatiously he took his service revolver from its holster and placed it on a table beside him.

'Sit down,' he ordered.

The man obeyed.

They waited in silence for several minutes. Then footsteps sounded on the stairs. The door opened widely, and Felicity appeared. A short, rotund man carrying a small briefcase followed her.

'Hallo, Doc,' smiled Dawlish, and then turned hard-faced towards the man opposite him. 'What was in the hypo?'

'Evipan,' the man muttered.

'We've a patient with a dose of evipan,' said Dawlish to Dr. Fraser. 'Just what does that mean?'

Until then the atmosphere in the room had been electric;

Fraser's arrival had not affected that, indeed, it had added to it. With the words, however, there was a change in the doctor's expression, and his answer eased the tension.

'That shouldn't cause much trouble,' he said confidently. 'I'll have a look at him, but he'll probably be round in half an hour. I suggest that you get some coffee ready, the patient will enjoy it when he comes round!' He went into the small bedroom, but was back in a matter of minutes. He turned to Dawlish with a reassuring nod. 'He'll be all right. In fact he ought to be round quite soon. How long has he been unconscious?'

'Fifteen or twenty minutes,' said Dawlish.

'Yes, I thought so. It wasn't too heavy a dose. Now do you want me, or am I in the way?'

Dr. Arnold Fraser had worked with and for Dawlish in the past; a man of admirable discretion, even in the days when Dawlish's activities had received no official blessing, he had been obliging and incurious. That was because Dawlish had taken him into his confidence to a limited degree; Fraser knew that sooner or later he would know just what was behind the urgent summons that evening.

'You're not exactly in the way,' said Dawlish, 'but—'

'All right, I get it,' said Fraser good-humouredly. 'Don't move, I'll let myself out.'

Dawlish smiled a goodbye, then stood up abruptly.

He was a large man, good-looking in a way, with an expression that could be deceptively wooden. Few would have imagined that he was considered good enough for the Intelligence Service, even the minor branch to which he was assigned; except the cynics, who would have declared that he was exactly the type with which Intelligence was crowded, unimaginative, quick perhaps in action but taking too long to reach decisions or react in emergency.

There they would have been wrong.

When Dawlish had first engaged, as he put it, in a little affair of crime, he had been, officially, unknown. Before it was finished Superintendent Trivett (then Chief Inspector) voiced the opinion that here was a mind which could think fast. Too fast, Trivett sometimes thought ruefully. In any event, Trivett was impressed. After that initial affair there had been others, but after a while Trivett and his superiors had found themselves asking Dawlish to help them in affairs which did not run true to criminal form.

At times he had worked not only against his own inclinations but also against Felicity's, the girl to whom he was engaged to be married, but when the war had started and he had ben drafted to Whitehall, Felicity had grown resigned to the inevitable.

Robbie Graham did not know that he was in 'Intelligence'.

The man sitting opposite Dawlish did not know it.

Felicity, of course, was well aware of it. She did not know how deep or how far the affair which had started that evening was to go, only that things which Dawlish started—or, as he declared, were started for him—had a habit of going a long way.

Nothing about the pallid face of the man with grey hair suggested that he would be easily persuaded to talk, but Felicity had recognised the method Dawlish was using, that of undermining his man's confidence.

Dawlish glanced up at her with a lop-sided smile.

'Lock yourself in with Robbie Graham, Fel, while I have a chat with this fellow, will you?'

Dawlish turned away from Felicity, and then looked into the grey-head's eyes.

CHAPTER TWO

GREY-HEAD DOESN'T KNOW

'For the past seventy-two hours,' said Dawlish without preamble, 'you have been following Lieutenant Graham, and you have made four attacks on his life. Why?'

The grey-head sat forward in his chair.

'You—you don't mean—'

'Let's get this straight,' said Dawlish harshly. 'I mean everything I say, including that I'm going to break your neck if I catch you out in a lie.' His expression was so fierce that he looked more than capable of carrying out the threat. 'You tried to kill him four times, and the fourth time I caught you. Why?'

Grey-head gulped.

'I had orders.'

'So you had orders,' said Dawlish scathingly. 'You were told to try to kill him, and you just said "yes sir", and off you started. Why, you bungling little amateur, do you think I'm going to believe that? Why do you want Graham dead?'

'It's true!' gasped the man. 'I was told to—to try to kill him. I don't know why. I never know why.'

'You never know why?' echoed Dawlish. He thrust his hands

deep into his pocket and leaned forward, thrusting his face close to the other's. 'What's your name?'

'B-Bateson.'

'Who gave you orders?'

Bateson swallowed again, and muttered:

'I—I had them by telephone.'

'So you're going to tell me that you can't say who gave the orders, or why they were given,' said Dawlish. 'I don't believe you, and I've told you what's going to happen if I consider you have lied to me.'

'It's true!' the man shouted. 'I took the message five days ago, I was told where to find Graham. I—I didn't argue, I couldn't argue.'

'Where did you first meet Graham?'

'At—at Liverpool.'

'Off his ship?'

'Yes.'

'So you were also told when he would reach England?'

'Yes,' said Bateson. 'They told me he'd arrive last Monday, that's all.'

'They told you when he would arrive and what you were to do to him,' said Dawlish. 'How often have you worked for "them"?'

Bateson said nothing.

'How often?' insisted Dawlish. There was a softer note in his voice, but he looked no less menacing. 'How often have you had commissions to murder? Is it your usual occupation, or just a sideline? Do you do it for pleasure or gain?'

Bateson reared back as Dawlish leaned further forward. He covered his face with his hands, as if anxious to evade the gaze from Dawlish's eyes.

Dawlish went on:

'What kind of story are you going to tell the police? How

many murders can they charge you with? *How long do you want to live, Bateson?'*

'Oh my God!' gasped Bateson. There was perspiration on his forehead, and his whole body was trembling. He cried defensibly: 'I've worked for them for a year or more, I haven't killed anybody, I've only frightened them. I can't help it, I have to do it. Let me go, let me get away from here!'

He made a movement from his chair.

Dawlish pressed a large hand against his chest and pushed him back.

'It's not going to be so easy,' he said. 'You've a lot more to talk about before you see the police. You've worked for someone for a year, and you don't know who it is? You've never made contact with any one of your employers? Come, Bateson, come, that won't keep you off the scaffold.'

'You can't have me hanged,' cried Bateson. 'I haven't killed anybody. I didn't kill Graham!'

'You did your damnedest,' said Dawlish. 'All right, I'll assume you've bungled everything you've tried. Who do you work for?'

Bateson began to gabble:

'I don't know any names. I've worked for them a year I tell you. They met me when I came out of Parkhurst, I hadn't anywhere to go, I was broke. They offered me a job and good money.' He stopped, gasping for breath, and then went on in the same high-pitched monotone: 'They send me messages by telephone, or they push them into my hand in the black-out. The only man I've ever seen is Kohn—he met me at Parkhurst—and now he's dead. The—the police got him.' He spat that sentence out, then went on at an even faster pace: 'How would you like to work that way?' He screamed at Dawlish, glaring wildly, his lips working and a few specks of froth at the corners of his mouth. 'How would you like it? Orders by phone, or something pushed into your hand. Do this, do that, threaten this man or that! I tell you I can't stand it any longer, I knew I shouldn't have tried to kill Graham, but they could send me down for a long stretch. I had to try!'

Perspiration streamed down his cheeks, into his distorted mouth. His hand was knocking against the arm of the chair, and his knees were shaking.

Slowly Dawlish's grim expression eased. He took out his cigarette-case, proffered it, and as Bateson took a cigarette he stepped aside and said:

'Would you like a drink?'

'Oh my God!' gasped Bateson. 'Yes, yes, I—'

His words faded away. He watched Dawlish wide-eyed as the large man poured out a whisky, added a touch of soda, and then carried it to his victim. Bateson drained it at a gulp, his violent fit of shaking lessening to occasional spasms.

'Another?'

'What—what are you playing at?' demanded Bateson shakily.

'Oddly enough, I feel sorry for you,' said Dawlish as he poured out another drink. 'Cause and effect hardly count. I can only deal with what I see, and I don't think you're as tough as you've tried to make out. Drink that more steadily,' he advised. 'That's better. Bateson, I gave you the choice of coming with me or going to the police. You chose wisely, for I might give you a break.'

Bateson stared, but said nothing.

'Write down the names and, where possible, the addresses of the people you've frightened,' said Dawlish. 'Give the dates of your efforts. Try to recall all details of telephone messages and other contacts. Write down your own name and address, and when you've done that I'll let you go.'

Bateson goggled at him.

'Let—let me go!'

'That's what I said,' repeated Dawlish.

'But—'

'Now come,' said Dawlish, 'don't look a gift horse in the mouth, it might bite you.' He shrugged his shoulders. 'I don't think I'm going to be interested in the little men of this show. If you've told the truth there are others far more important than you. I want them.'

Dawlish turned towards another door, which opened into a dining-room, and said: 'Come in here.'

Bateson followed him. Dawlish put pen and ink, paper and a blotting pad on the dining-table, then stepped to the window, pushed it up and set the catch.

'If you try to get out before you've finished I'll change my mind,' he said affably. 'There's a burglar alarm at the window, and if you move it the whole building will be roused.'

He went out and closed the door.

He stood ruminating for some seconds, then shrugged his shoulders and pulled the curtains aside. Two or three people were walking along the street, but no one appeared to take any particular notice of Number 88g.

'I wish Ted would come,' he said audibly. 'He's probably at Freddy's, drat him.'

Dawlish waited for another five minutes, then saw the tall, khaki-clad figure of Ted Beresford walking along the street.

Dawlish opened the door as Ted's footsteps sounded on the landing.

On closer inspection his friend was seen to be a plain man, easily redeemed by his brown eyes and dazzling teeth.

'Hallo, hallo, what's got into you, Pat? I haven't seen you looking so grim for a long time. Temperature all right? Sore throat? Thick head?'

'There's no time for persiflage,' said Dawlish firmly. 'We're on to something.'

Ted stared. 'Us? No!'

'Us. Yes. A case has been dropped into our laps. For four months we've meandered about Westminister doing damn all, and now we've got something right on the doorstep.'

'Well, I'm darned!' exclaimed Ted. 'So down in Whitehall something has stirred at last. It would come to you and not to me, wouldn't it? Who started the hare? Old Whitewash?'

'So far it's unofficial,' Dawlish told him.

Beresford's expression altered, his voice grew deeper. 'Are you serious, Pat? I thought you were joking.'

'It's serious,' Dawlish assured him. 'Robbie Graham poured apparent gibberish in my ear, and by the grace of God and an inquisitive mind, I listened. Also—but let's tell Robbie and Felicity as well,' he added.

He stepped across the room to the telephone. 'Who's in town, and living near by? It's a pity Tim's not here but—ah, Tony will do,' he added abruptly, and lifted the receiver.

Ted waited and watched while he dialled a number, and listened while Dawlish said:

'Is Captain Grayling in? . . . Hallo, Tony, are you busy? . . . Good man. You know the hole which used to be a house at the back of my place? . . . Yes, that's it, you can get there from your flat easily enough. Go and stand by there for half an hour, will you, it's just possible I'll be having a visitor. What's that? . . . Just as soon as I can. I'll tell you what it's about later, but now I'm in a hurry. Cheers.'

He rang off, and contemplated Ted.

'Obliging friends, yours,' said Ted. 'I'm burned up with curiosity.'

It was then that the spare-room door opened, and Felicity

looked through. Over her shoulder Dawlish could see Robbie sitting on the bed, his face pale, his hair standing up on end.

'I can't keep him there much longer,' said Felicity.

'Let him out,' smiled Dawlish.

'What I like about this affair,' declared Beresford, 'is the nice, homely atmosphere, not to speak of the clear and concise way in which you're telling the story, Patrick. I—'

'*Now!*' exclaimed Robbie vigorously. 'What is it all about?'

'Mostly you,' said Dawlish. 'You started it, you know.'

'Started what?' Robbie entered the lounge as Ted dropped into a chair and Felicity pulled up another. 'So you *did* take me seriously?'

Dawlish chuckled.

'I wasn't as uninterested as I seemed, Robbie. I was in the smoking-room when you came in, remember? I saw a man following you in a rather too casual manner, and I wondered why. Also he was a stranger, and I'm suspicious of strange faces in the Carilon.'

Robbie stared at him, then walked to a chair and sat down.

'When you'd told me the sad story,' continued Dawlish, 'I thought it odd. You wouldn't talk like that without good reason. If you had been attacked, then you had been followed several times. Why not again? I decided to take no notice of what you said, but pass it off. I did. You went. The stranger followed you and I followed the stranger. On the bridge, you may, or may not, remember there was a spot of bother.'

Robbie swallowed hard.

'Bother,' he murmured. 'Bother! A swan!'

'Now don't you start,' implored Beresford.

'I'm not starting,' said Robbie. 'I was looking over into the river and this swab came along and began burbling about swans. Then he jabbed a pin into me, and I thought he was going to pitch me over the bridge. I—but you turned up then, Dawlish.'

'I was around,' admitted Dawlish.

He told them what had happened, including much of his interview with the man who called himself Bateson. None of them interrupted, although once or twice Robbie opened his lips.

From time to time Beresford smiled; each time the smile gave an impression of deeper contentment.

'And so,' finished Dawlish, 'I telephoned Tony Grayling, just in case anyone should have followed me, and decided to try to influence Bateson. I think, at the moment, he's writing up the history of his past twelve months. Not a nice little man, but frightened.'

'You're a heartless beast,' Felicity assured him.

'My sweet!' exclaimed Dawlish reproachfully. 'Remember what he was trying to do.'

'It hasn't really registered,' admitted Felicity, whose grey-green eyes held a hint of bewilderment. 'How could he expect to throw Robbie over the bridge in broad daylight, and then get away? And even if he did, Robbie can swim.'

'Johnny Weismuller can swim too, but if he'd been dosed with evipan, a drug guaranteed to put you out in a few seconds and leave you that way for half an hour, Johnny wouldn't have lived to tell the tale.'

'I feel perfectly all right,' protested Robbie. 'I can't really believe that I've been out.'

'I know this is a jolly world,' said Dawlish, 'and that the one thing we all like to hear is the next man or woman saying he can't believe it, but let's deal in facts. It all happened. Robbie would have been drowned, and there was a sound chance that it would have been listed as "accidental death".'

'I say!' said Robbie hollowly. 'I don't like the sound of that.' He paused.

'Well, let's hear some tangible reason for the attacks on you,' urged Dawlish. 'There've been four, including one in a country lane.'

'It nearly finished me,' declared Robbie. 'I was on a bike, you know, tooling along doing no harm to anybody, when suddenly I found myself hustled into a ditch! There was no sense in it.'

'Of course there was sense in it,' insisted Dawlish. 'Things like that don't happen without a purpose. Bateson—he's the evipan johnny—says that he was told what ship you'd be on, and when you were berthing in Liverpool. Not many people should know troop movements, so we know that Bateson's employers are well informed, and that they want Robert McEwart Graham dead,' said Dawlish. 'That is the effect. What do you know of the cause, Robbie?'

'*Absolutely* nothing at all!' declared Robbie roundly. 'I don't really know why I'm in England. It wasn't ordinary leave, I was just told I was being moved. I get used to mysterious comings and goings; you know what I mean. Mine not to reason why, mine just to come and go. I wasn't sorry to get back for a bit, but—damn it, why was I sent here?'

'That's what we want to know,' said Dawlish.

CHAPTER THREE

FOLLOW MR. BATESON

Robbie could venture no guess at the reason for his transfer.

'Bateson's list might tell us something,' said Dawlish. 'What's that, Fel?'

Felicity was frowning. 'Pat, oughtn't you to send Bateson to the police?'

'I'd been wondering that,' put in Robbie.

'I know you'd like to handle it yourself,' went on Felicity quietly, 'but is it wise?' She met Dawlish's eyes squarely. 'What I mean is,' she continued quietly, 'that you mustn't let the last few months of sitting around make you do something which might lead to trouble at the office.'

'Agreed,' said Dawlish. 'But I needn't take the police into our confidence yet. Knowing what I can tell them, they'd detain Bateson. We don't want Bateson detained.'

'It doesn't seem such a bad idea,' said Robbie earnestly.

Dawlish chuckled.

'You'll get over the symptoms, old son. Now come, obviously we want Bateson followed, and we *are* attached to "Intelligence".'

'I'd got that fact,' said Felicity, 'but I don't see how it can help.

He doesn't know anyone, he says, he just waits for a contact out of the blue, and then does what he's told. Aren't you going to waste time following him?'

'I'm not going to follow him,' declared Dawlish, 'Beresford is. Bateson himself was probably followed. Presuming that there is an organisation on the lines he's suggested, and I don't think he's lying, his movements would be watched. The real men behind the attacks would keep at a safe distance but have the satisfaction of knowing when their job's done. Consequently it's probably known that Bateson's here, and there's a chance that he'll be followed when he goes. So Ted keeps on his tail, and if anything does break, we'll be in on the ground floor.'

'Mixed metaphors apart, that's all right,' decided Beresford. 'What other dark doings are you contemplating, Pat?'

Dawlish rubbed his nose thoughtfully.

'First, tell the Boss. Second, try to make head or tail of Bateson's list, and third, try to find some reason for the attacks on Robbie. Although Bateson's out, Robbie isn't necessarily off the casualty list, so he'd better stay here for a bit and look after you, Fel.' He paused, and then asked: 'Any complaints?'

'Not from me,' said Robbie warmly.

There was a general chuckle, and Dawlish went into the dining-room.

Bateson was sitting back in his chair. Several sheets of paper were lying face downwards on the table. He looked up when Dawlish appeared, and exclaimed:

'You weren't lying? You'll let me go?'

'You really want to go?' asked Dawlish.

Bateson pushed his chair back and stood up. His face was flushed, his eyes glittering. 'You told me you'd let me go. If the police get me it'll mean a long stretch.'

Dawlish smiled. 'A deal's a deal. You're as free as the air. Or you will be in five minutes.'

He went to the window and looked towards the rubble of the blitzed houses. A solitary figure in khaki leaned against an iron girder. Dawlish pushed the window up, and whistled.

Tony Grayling looked up with a start.

Dawlish beckoned him. Tony started to move towards the house, and Dawlish closed the window, turning back to the lounge. Ted was standing by the door, his hat in his hand, stick and gloves with it.

'Yes?' he asked.

'Yes,' said Dawlish. 'Take care of yourself.'

Beresford grinned, blew a kiss to Felicity, and then left the flat.

Five minutes later, Bateson left.

Dawlish took him down to the street, delivering a harangue which, he knew, would do no good, at the same time covering Beresford's first movement in the little man's wake.

Dawlish watched them out of sight.

When he reached the flat again, Tony Grayling was entering by way of the rear entrance. A man three inches short of Dawlish's six-feet odd, Grayling was dark, clear-cut, almost saturnine of features. He lifted a hand in greeting.

'I was just wondering where you'd got to. What's to do, Pat? More tricks?'

'You could call it that,' said Dawlish with a grin. 'Thanks for getting on to the job, Tony. How long are you on leave?'

'I've five days left.'

'Can you spare the evening?'

'Yes, if it's for anything worth while.'

'Well, I can't guarantee anything, but it could be lively. I'm going along to see my Guv'nor, and there's a chance I might be followed.'

'I'm on,' said Grayling. 'May I use your phone?'

'Go ahead,' said Dawlish. He slipped an arm about Felicity's shoulder, and led her to the kitchen. Once there, he turned and faced her, smiling a little.

Felicity was not smiling when she said:

'Am I too much possessive, Pat?'

'My sweet, I know just how you feel,' protested Dawlish.

'Sometimes I wonder if you do,' said Felicity. 'When anything like this starts I feel cold and dead inside. And I can't breathe freely until it's over. I suppose—' She paused, but Dawlish did not interrupt her, and she went on: 'I suppose it's because I'm so damnably afraid that one of them will kill you.'

Dawlish stooped a little and kissed the end of her nose.

'That's not being possessive, it's love. I feel the same about you.'

'Ye-es,' said Felicity. She forced a smile. 'You think you're on to something, don't you?'

'It has the makings of quite a show, yes,' said Dawlish. 'The precautions which Bateson's boy-friends take to keep under cover aren't exactly unique, but they're pretty comprehensive. Someone behind this has a mind.' He kissed her again, this time not so lightly, and gripped her shoulders. 'You're not forgetting, are you, that I might be abroad?'

'No,' said Felicity. 'But this could be worse. Robbie's been through a lot in Libya, but this scares *him*.'

Dawlish chuckled.

'Only because he's not used to it. In any case,' he went on, 'it might prove nothing at all, and Whitewash might tell me to stick to my desk and mind my own business.'

'He won't do anything of the kind, and you know it.'

He gave her a bear-like hug, and they returned to the others.

With Grayling Dawlish left the flat soon afterwards, turning right when he reached Jermyn Street. The quicker route to the home of his Chief was to the left, but if he were followed he wanted to give his trailer plenty of time to operate in, and himself time to see what was happening.

Consequently he started off in the same direction that Beresford and Bateson had taken.

Ted Beresford was not thinking of anything but his immediate task as he followed his man.

Beresford himself would have been the first to admit that he was not a creative member of the community. He did not like giving orders, preferring to take them—within limits. He knew as well as Dawlish that he lacked initiative, but when given a job to do he was excelled by few.

He was the only one of Dawlish's friends who had been with their leader through every adventure. He knew Dawlish surprisingly well, aware of both his qualities and his shortcomings, and was prepared to trust him with devotion and loyalty.

In this instance he did not ask himself whether Dawlish was expecting too much of the affair, or whether he had been wise to allow Bateson to go; he just followed Bateson.

In Piccadilly his quarry went down into a sub-way. Beresford followed, pushing aside several people in his haste, heedless of indignant reproaches. The roundabout beneath Piccadilly Circus was a dangerous place for losing a man, and Beresford wanted nothing to go wrong.

In Jermyn Street he had noticed a second man.

Except that the second worthy had started to move in Bateson's wake, there was nothing outstanding about him. He was a middle-aged fellow in a shabby suit, and he walked with a slouch. Beresford saw him again beneath Piccadilly. Bateson was buying a ticket at one of the machines marked 3d.

The shabby man and Beresford also bought 3d. tickets.

They hurried in Bateson's wake, down the escalators, and along the sub-way to a platform where a dozen people were waiting. In the distance a train rumbled through the tunnel.

Beresford stayed among the crowd. Bateson walked a few yards along, never going too close to the edge. He took a loose cigarette from his breast-pocket, lit it from a book of matches, and watched the train approaching. The crowd surged towards it as it ran into the platform.

The shabby man moved swiftly, and drew alongside Bateson.

Then and then only did Beresford see Bateson's danger. He shouted, but his voice was lost in the rumbling of the train.

The shabby man lunged against Bateson.

Beresford sprang forward in a desperate attempt to save Bateson, but the man lost his footing and pitched on to the line.

There was a vivid flash, a sudden, horrible smell of burning. The brakes of the train screeched, lights flickered and then went out. A strange, uncanny silence lasted for a few seconds before a woman began to scream.

CHAPTER FOUR

DAWLISH AROUSES INTEREST

Beresford heard the scream. A man shouted for 'lights', and a rougher voice boomed:

'Stay where you are, everyone!'

The advice was not heeded.

Beresford saw people moving. From beyond the exit archway a light was coming. He saw a uniformed man hurrying along, and then a shadowy figure rush from the platform towards the station official.

'*If* you please,' said the latter, and stretched out a hand to stop the man.

A swinging blow in the stomach doubled him up. The assailant could only be the shabby man, the one who had pushed Bateson under the oncoming train, and Beresford rushed forward in his wake.

Behind them gates clanged; they were the entrance gates, closed in the emergency.

Doggedly following his quarry, Beresford struggled through the crowd. When he reached the foot of the escalator his man was near the top. Beresford started up, two steps at a time, then heard a shout from below.

He did not look round.

The guard who had been floored by the shabby one was at the foot of the escalator. He shouted a second time, when Beresford was no more than half-way up the stairs. Then he smashed the glass of the contraption at the foot of the escalator, pressed the brass knob inside, and stood staring upwards with grim satisfaction.

The escalator stopped with a jerk.

'So that's that,' he thought sourly. 'Now I suppose I'll have to answer shoals of questions.'

The guard reached him and put a heavy hand on his shoulder.

Beresford eyed him sombrely, seeing a leathery face and hostile eyes. He no longer felt sorry for the guard; he wished the man to perdition, for without him the shabby man would have been followed. Now the chase was futile, and Dawlish would be disappointed. Dawlish must have expected just such a tragedy as this, and had sent Beresford to save the little man from the expected vengeance.

'You can save your explanation for the police,' the guard adjured him grimly, 'and now git orf the staircase, we want to start it again.'

Outside a house in Audeley Street, Dawlish and Grayling stopped walking and regarded one another in the failing light. Grayling said testily:

'I thought you'd got something for me to do, I didn't expect a gentle stroll. I'd a pleasant evening in prospect, too.'

'We haven't collected any broken heads yet,' Dawlish admitted, 'but we may do before the night's out. Do you feel like hanging around until I've finished with Whitewash?'

'Do you expect ructions?'

Dawlish shrugged. 'Who knows? I'm steeled against surprise of any kind.'

'Brave words. I may live to see you eat them,' Grayling assured him.

Dawlish smiled, and stepped into the porch of Number 47a. Passing through the brilliantly lit hall, he heard the strains of piano music against a background of conversation and laughter.

He remembered that his chief, Colonel Arbuthnot Whitehead, O.B.E., M.C., was given to parties. Dawlish had attended many of them, and knew that they always had a purpose other than mere entertainment. Whitehead's position in the Intelligence Department was not well-defined, however, and by many he was looked upon as a relic of the bad, or good, old days, according to one's outlook. There had been veiled comments in the press about his 'gatherings', particularly on the grounds that there was much waste of money, too much food, and completely unnecessary frivolity. To all such criticism Whitehead turned a bland countenance.

He was a bland gentleman.

Tall, pale-faced, his eyes were a light grey, always half-covered by heavy lids. He had earned the soubriquet of 'Whitewash' from a trait which all the members of his staff appreciated, although outsiders commented unfavourably upon it. If things went wrong in his Department, Whitehead took the blame. He had been known to enter a passionate defence of a member of his staff, and then call the member up and talk to him to such effect that the unfortunate shivered when he recalled the interview.

From a narrow staircase the Colonel approached Dawlish.

'Hallo, my dear fellow. Nice of you to look in tonight.'

'I'd like a few words with you,' said Dawlish. 'I sent word by phone.'

Whitehead regarded him narrowly. 'Piloski is about to give a recital. I thought that had brought you! I'll be at the office in the morning, of course.'

'I don't think this will keep until morning,' insisted Dawlish.

He knew as well as Whitehead that the reception was no more and no less than a meeting of people who might give information, or might be in a position to obtain it. Thus, under the facade of gaiety and frivolity much good work was done.

Dawlish had little to do with those activities.

Whitehead had once dubbed him his first reserve, to be called on if anything happened in England which needed quick and ruthless action. Now, eyeing him narrowly, he said:

'Well, if you really think it's important, come up to my room.'

In his study, he took whisky and soda from a cupboard in his desk and pushed a box of cigarettes across to Dawlish.

'Well, sit down. It won't take too long, I hope.'

'I'll cut the introduction as short as I can. You should know first that I knew nothing of this business until this evening.'

Whitehead smiled.

'Right. Now we've established that fact, go on.'

Dawlish condensed his story into ten minutes.

Throughout the narration, Whitehead peered at him through half-closed eyes, occasionally toying with the whisky decanter.

'That's pretty well as much as I can tell you, sir. I may have some news from Beresford later.'

'Ye-es,' said Whitehead. 'I can see that. Y'know, Dawlish, I haven't been so interested in a story for a long time. I should have felt very annoyed had you waited until the morning before coming to tell me.' He smiled. 'What we need to know is whether there was any particular reason for Graham's return, which might give us a motive for the attacks on him. Have you got the list of people whom this fellow Bateson has—er—frightened?'

Dawlish took the sheets of paper from his pocket.

'I haven't read it yet,' he said. 'I thought you'd like to see it first.'

'That's very thoughtful of you.' Whitehead took the papers. 'You'll have a drink?'

'Thanks.'

Bateson's statement was read without haste.

From downstairs there came the occasional strains of music, once or twice a burst of applause.

Dawlish reflected that it was the first time he had made contact with anything which looked interesting while working for Whitehead, and that he had been wise to adopt this method of approach. He did not find it easy. In the past he had been brought in as a special agent, and had been able to make his own conditions, working as he thought best. Now it was likely that he would be hedged about by orders and provisos.

Whitehead finished at last and dropped the paper to his desk.

'Even more interesting,' he acknowledged. 'He names eight people, but I don't recognise any of them. However, that doesn't mean a great deal. Take this with you, and get some copies made, will you? Let me have three—no, four—in the morning, and keep as many as you want yourself. Now, what do you suggest about Graham? Anything of particular interest about him?'

'If there is he's kept it covered very well,' said Dawlish. 'I'd say that he was a good man, a little on the naïve side. Nothing very deep, but sound enough.'

'But they did bring him back from Libya.'

'Can *you* find out why, sir?' asked Dawlish.

'I can have a good try,' Whitehead assured him. 'Yes, a very good try. Well, Dawlish, it looks as if you're going to have your wish for something to do.' He chuckled. 'I've been watching you and Beresford. Fishes out of water, of course; how you hate being desk-bound! The penalty of a reputation, you know, you've made some of us think that it's much better to have you at hand. I'm one of them.' He paused.

'That's good of you,' said Dawlish, surprised.

'Nonsense!' Whitehead with unexpected vehemence. 'We also know that you don't like being shackled. No doubt you've been sitting there telling yourself that you're going to be hedged about by this and that. Don't you believe it. I'll get all the information I can, and I'll pass it on to you. I'll send a chit through to the police telling them what you're up to. You know them fairly well, don't you?'

'Yes,' said Dawlish, now less surprised than astonished.

'Good, then they won't give you any trouble. Now I don't know what this is about any more than you do, but I'm going to be surprised if we don't know a lot more before the week's out. You'll want Beresford, of course. Anyone else?'

Dawlish swallowed.

'Graham might be useful,' he said. 'And I'd rather like to have Tim Jeremy. He's still with his unit, but it's in Surrey. He's used to—'

'Working with you, yes. All right, I'll see what I can do.' Whitehead sipped his drink. 'You know what your position is, and you know you can ask me for help as well as the police, if you think it's necessary. Right you are, then, off you go and good luck. I'll just have time to hear the last twenty minutes of Piloski. You won't mind if I hurry away? Goodnight, Dawlish, goodnight.'

The Colonel opened the door and hurried through ahead of Dawlish. In a much happier mood than when he had arrived Dawlish tucked Bateson's statement into his pocket and made his way to the hall. No servant was there, and he let himself out.

A dark figure materialised out of the gloom, the shape of his peaked hat just visible.

'Hallo, Tony,' said Dawlish cheerfully. 'We're going to be busy after all.'

He stopped abruptly.

The grunt of response was followed by the upward movement of the man's arm. Dawlish side-stepped sharply as a blow whistled past his head.

He drove a punch towards the man's stomach.

His assailant had expected the blow, and evaded it. Another blow at Dawlish missed by a fraction; but suddenly he found himself assailed on all sides.

He heard footsteps, but saw nothing except the pale blurs of faces. Blows fell on his head and shoulders, making him gasp with pain. He backed slowly into the porch.

Something light, almost feathery, smacked against his face. There was a little 'pop' and a tinkle of glass, then a gust of acrid-smelling stuff in his nostrils. He thought 'gas', and fumbled desperately in his pocket, until his fingers found and clutched Bateson's paper. He screwed it up into a ball and flicked it ahead of him, over the heads of his assailants.

Then something seemed to explode in his head, and he lost consciousness.

He did not know how long he was unconscious. When he came round his eyes were smarting and there was an unpleasant sensation in his head. He saw a vague blur of a face near him, and a bright light. The light hurt his eyes, and he muttered:

'Put the light out. Put it out.'

Someone spoke.

Through the fumes of semi-consciousness Dawlish's mind began to work. He remembered the attack and what had preceded it, even his own effort for the paper. He had just time to wonder whether he was with friends when the light went out.

A dimmer one replaced it.

'How are you, Dawlish?' asked Whitehead.

Dawlish drew a deep breath of relief. He realised that he was lying on a bed. His collar and tie were loose, his shoes were off, but otherwise he was fully clad. He remembered Robbie Graham in a like plight; and then thought of Tony.

'Colonel! Captain Grayling, he—'

'All right, all right,' said Whitehead gruffly. 'We've found him, and he's not badly hurt. Stop worrying. Dawlish, which pocket did you put those papers in?'

Dawlish struggled to a sitting position as a door opened and a maid brought in a tray. Whitehead poured him out some coffee.

'Thanks. I screwed the papers up into a ball and tossed them into the street. I doubt if I was seen.'

'Well I'm damned!' exclaimed Whitehead.

He went to the door, giving rapid instructions. When he returned he was smiling a little.

'That was smart,' he admitted. 'We heard the shout, and when we found you they'd taken everything from your coat pockets. Just what happened?'

With the coffee warming him, and the hammering in his head much easier, Dawlish reported everything he remembered. Finished, he learned that it was ten minutes to eleven, and that Tony Grayling had been found unconscious in the porch next door. He prevailed upon Whitehead to telephone his flat with the assurance that he was all right but would be late, and then reviewed the situation.

A doctor, brought to see him and Tony, reported that Tony's condition might have been caused by evipan, and Dawlish said:

'Probably it was, the stuff has been used once in this show. The thing I can't understand is why they chose to clout me over the head, instead of pumping the stuff into me. There wouldn't have been a chance then.' He paused and looked into Whitehead's face. 'One of the enemy's mistakes, I suppose, but it's odd. Well, it looks as if someone thinks that paper is important. I hope to heaven you find it.'

Whitehead frowned. 'They should have done so by now.'

But they were not back in another ten minutes, and by then Dawlish and Whitehead were growing perturbed. Dawlish insisted that he was well enough to join in the search, and together they went into Audeley Street.

There they saw a scene which might have made them laugh in different circumstances.

Eight or nine torches were shining towards the kerb, and against their light the legs of eight or nine men moved. Sometimes a head bobbed down and showed in silhouette, or else a hand stretched towards the pavement and was withdrawn quickly.

Suddenly a gust of wind howled along the street.

It was unexpected, for the night had been calm. The gust rattled against windows, and made Dawlish catch his breath. It lasted for perhaps ten seconds and then died away. Dawlish was scowling at the torches, and heard a man say:

'If we have many of those we won't find no paper.'

'No,' said Dawlish aloud. 'Colonel, eight men are no use, we want a couple of dozen, and we daren't wait until daylight. Will you see what you can do?'

His words were cut short by another gust of wind. Dust stung his eyes, and collected on his lips. He had an uneasy fear that the wind might do what his assailants had failed to achieve.

CHAPTER FIVE

FIRST ON THE LIST

The local A.R.P. workers on duty, a band of fire-watchers, and several policemen joined in the search. Audeley Street was ablaze with torches and criss-crossed with shadows. The search went on until nearly one o'clock.

By then Dawlish had forgotten his misadventure, and was thinking only of the paper.

Tony Grayling had recovered and joined in. Whitehead himself walked up and down the street asking frequent questions. The streets bisecting the thoroughfare had their quota of searchers, and it soon grew obvious that if they were to find the paper they would be lucky.

Then Whitehead said:

'It looks as if they might have picked it up, Dawlish.'

'That's what's worrying me,' said Dawlish, 'but they couldn't have known that I had the list.'

'They might have taken a chance that you had something,' said Whitehead. 'I—what's that?'

From somewhere along the street came a positive 'view hallo!' followed by hurrying footsteps. Dawlish and Whitehead went to meet a policeman who was holding a torch in one hand and a screw of paper in the other.

'This looks like it, sir,' he said eagerly.

Dawlish took the ball quickly, smoothed it out, and in the light of the policeman's torch recognised Bateson's handwriting. He drew a deep breath of relief and took out a couple of crumpled pound notes which his assailants had left in his trousers pocket.

'Constable,' he said, 'it's more than worth it.'

'Oh no, sir,' said the constable quickly, 'I couldn't—'

'Hush,' said Dawlish. 'Don't tell the world.'

The man murmured thanks, and stowed the notes away.

Dawlish and Whitehead moved back to the house, their one thought being to get the list duplicated before further mishaps.

Dawlish tapped inexpertly on a portable typewriter, confident that it would be unwise to have a typist work on it.

The names meant no more to him than they did to Whitehead, although by the time he had finished he knew them off by heart. They were:

(1) Mr. James Rennett, 18a The Grove, Westbourne.

(2) Mr. Arthur Train, 23 Lime Street, Fulham.

(3) Mr. Jacob Rosstein, Lintara, Elm Street, Hampstead.

(4) Mr. George Edward Cornwallis, Little Granley, Surrey.

(5) Mrs. Elizabeth Arthurson, 9 Linden Drive, Dorchester.

(6) Mrs. Benn, 91 Leston Bridge Road, Ewell, Surrey.

(7) Mr. Hennessy, The Lees, Near Wimborne, Dorset.

(8) Dr. Arnold Pollittzer, Poole, Dorset.

In addition to the names and addresses there were approximate dates of the attempts to 'frighten' the people mentioned, and there was a list of the places where Bateson had met members of the organisation. There was some mention also, of a Gabriel Kohn, who had been charged soon afterwards with black market work, and had killed himself.

'Kohn's record might help,' said Dawlish, and yawned. 'Well, there are four copies, anyhow.'

The carbon copies of the list were liberally dotted with smudges where he had rubbed out, but he did not let that worry him. He addressed one to himself, at his flat and one to the office, put the third in his pocket with the original, and the fourth copy he left with Whitehead.

Tony had already returned to Jermyn Street. Whitehead, whose eyes drooped with fatigue, and whose guests had long since departed, shook hands and told him that he hoped it would not be long before he had something of his revenge. He also exhorted Dawlish to be careful.

Dawlish chuckled about that as he walked home.

Robbie and Tony were dozing in easy chairs, and Felicity was lying on the spare-room bed with her shoes off. Dawlish saw her head against the pillow as he entered the flat, and raised a hand towards the others for silence. He walked softly across to the bedroom door and looked down. Felicity was sleeping soundly, her hair spread about the pillow.

He smiled and closed the door.

It was a quarter to three, and all of them were tired. Grayling was anxious to get back to his flat, but equally anxious to hear from Ted Beresford.

Dawlish frowned.

'Hasn't he telephoned?'

'Not a word.'

'If these johnnies are going to carry on the way they've started, we won't be safe unless we go about with a suit of mail and a gas-mask,' said Robbie. 'Y'know, Dawlish, I still haven't taken it all in. I mean, an attack on you in Audeley Street. Damn it, do things like that happen?'

'Hearken to the innocent,' said Dawlish. 'They do; they did. Don't get the "it-can't-happen-here" complex, Robbie. The only reason why similar things don't happen often is lack of sufficient motive. To take a big risk the motive has to be big.' He broke off, frowning. 'I wish there was a word from Ted.'

'Is it any use phoning the police?' asked Grayling.

'Nothing is any good,' said Dawlish. 'If he's been in touch with the police he'll get word through to us through the Yard sooner or later. If he hasn't—'

Grayling left soon afterwards, declaring that he would get safely to his flat if it took him an hour. Dawlish went downstairs with him.

Returning, he found Robbie half asleep in an easy chair. He struggled up to a sitting position.

'Are we keeping a watch, old man?'

'No,' said Dawlish. 'We're locking the doors and windows, they're fitted with an alarm system that's pretty well foolproof. Not that I expect anything else to happen tonight.'

'You can't be sure.'

'Let's not meet trouble half-way. What are you going to do?'

'I was going to stay at the club,' admitted Robbie, 'but there's not much left of the night. Can I shake-down with you?'

Dawlish said that he could, gladly.

In the main bedroom there were twin beds, and as they undressed Robbie grew more wakeful. He continued from where he had left off in the Carilon Club. After the shooting in the country lane he had felt jumpy, he said, and, not wanting to worry his family, had faked an excuse for returning to London.

'What part of the country is it?' asked Dawlish.

'Near Wimborne,' said Robbie. 'Dorset, you know.'

Dawlish stiffened.

'It's a darned fine county,' Robbie went on, with a flash of pride in his native soil. 'It doesn't get shouted about like some of the others, but you'll have to go a long way to beat it for scenery.'

Dawlish said slowly:

'Of the names and addresses which Bateson gave us, three were in Dorset and two in Surrey. The rest were in London.'

Robbie stopped turning down the sheet.

'That's odd.'

'Odd's the word,' said Dawlish. 'Do you know a place called The Lees?'

'The Lees?' Robbie stared at him, his chubby face suddenly tense. 'Why, of course. It's old Hennessy's place. Big house, not far from Wimbourne. Pretty much of a recluse, and not over-popular at the moment.'

'Why is that?'

'He's too damned anti-war,' declared Robbie. 'As a matter of fact he and his only son had a hell of a row just after things started. I knew Dick Hennessy pretty well,' he added. 'He had a yacht in peace time, and they grabbed him when he volunteered for the Navy. There was a bust-up, the old boy wanted him to wait until he was called up and then declare that he didn't believe in war. I say, Dawlish, is Hennessy really on the list?'

'He is,' said Dawlish. 'Do you happen to have heard of a Mrs. Arthurson, of Dorchester?'

Robbie sat heavily on the side of the bed.

'Everyone knows Lizzie! Don't tell me she's on it!'

'She is.'

'But it's so damned silly!' exclaimed Robbie. 'She organises this and that up and down the county, getting everybody working whether they want to or not. You know the kind. As a matter of fact'—Robbie ran a hand bewilderedly through his curly hair—'as a matter of fact there was some talk once that she and Hennessy would get married. She's a widow touching sixty, but youngish. But about a year ago I heard that everything was off between her and Hennessy, presumably because of his pacifism. I say, Dawlish, what does this mean?'

Dawlish said: 'Hold tight, Robbie. What about Pollittzer, doctor, of Poole?'

Robbie gasped: '*Polly!* Polly's on the list?'

'You can't know him,' protested Dawlish faintly.

'Don't be an ass. Everyone knows Polly. Everyone in Dorset, that is. He digs for things.'

'Digs?' murmured Dawlish.

'You know, flints and Roman coins. Nicest old boy you'll find in a month of Sundays. He goes round all the towns and villages giving talks on the history of Dorset. Folklore stuff.' Robbie passed a hand through his already upstanding hair. 'Is *he* on the list'?

'He's Number 8. Bateson had a go at him six months ago.'

'But look here, no one *could* frighten Polly. They didn't have a good time in Poole during the worst of the blitz period, you know, and he was always in the thick of it. He was a G.P. but retired ages ago. He did some more digging in the blitzed places down there, and got something for it—M.B.E., I think. Mother was talking about it the last time I was home.'

Before Robbie could go on there was a ring at the front door.

It startled them, until Dawlish said: 'That's Ted,' and dashed out eagerly. His arrival in the hall coincided with Felicity's, tired and sleepy eyed.

As Dawlish turned the knob of the door it occurred to him that he might be wrong, and find someone else outside. He was not; for Ted came in with a rueful grin on his face, his hair dishevelled.

He tossed his hat on to a chair resignedly.

'Well, folks,' he said. 'Kick me for the worst of bunglers.'

'Trouble?' asked Dawlish quietly.

'Pretty bad,' admitted Beresford. 'Bateson's dead, and I lost the cove who killed him.'

Robbie came from the room with a voluminous dressing-gown wrapped about him. Dawlish wore only his pyjamas. Beresford loosened his collar, dropped into an easy chair, and went through his story.

'After the guard had stopped the escalator I had the devil's own job,' he said finally. 'Two or three people thought they'd seen Bateson pushed, and in the confusion they decided that I was the pusher. The lights went out, as I've told you, and I was seen running away. There was a shindy on the platform with people fainting all over the place. Getting Bateson off the line wasn't so good, either.' Beresford scowled and looked at the ceiling. 'I didn't know what to do, Pat. I didn't want to drag you into the affair, or say anything about the office, so I held tight and asked for Trivett. They took me along to the nearest police station. Trivett wasn't there, of course, but he turned up at last and gave me all the help I wanted. He's coming round in the morning.'

Dawlish nodded.

'You didn't get a good look at the shabby man, I suppose?'

'Not what you'd call a good look,' admitted Beresford. 'It was pretty dark, and I only saw his back and a glimpse or two of his profile. He's one of those difficult coves to sum up. Vague kind of johnny. I'd recognise him again, but it wouldn't be easy to give a description. Sorry, old man, for bungling it.'

'Don't be an ass,' said Dawlish. 'You came out of it darned well.'

By the time he had told Beresford what else had happened it had turned four o'clock. Beresford, who shared the flat with

Dawlish, decided to sleep in an easy chair. Felicity, who had a small flat near by but was often at Jermyn Street, went back to the spare room. She said little, but Dawlish imagined that she would be awake for some time.

Heavily though he slept, he awakened just after eight o'clock next morning.

By half past eight Felicity was preparing breakfast and the men were arguing about the right to shave first.

At half past nine they were all washed and shaved, and breakfast was finished. Robbie offered to help with the washing up, and there was a clatter in the kitchen when a ring at the front door heralded Superintendent Trivett, of Scotland Yard.

An old friend of Dawlish's and Beresford's, tall, dark, and more than passably good-looking, Trivett told them that he had received orders from the Chief Constable to give Dawlish all the help he could.

'So Whitehead doesn't lose time,' reflected Dawlish. 'Are you busy, Bill?'

Trivett looked at him intently.

'Busy enough. Why?'

'I'm going down to Dorset to look up one or two people. It might be useful to have you around.'

Trivett shook his head.

'You should know better than that, Pat. I'd have to get in touch with the Dorset people, and they'd probably be a bit put out if I simply gate-crashed. But I'll give you some introductions, and if you'll let me have a copy of that list I'll find out what I can about the people on it. Will that help?'

Beresford said eagerly: 'Pat, I'll come down to Dorset with you, let Bill look after the London end for a while.'

'I was thinking of going home for a day or two,' said Robbie pointedly.

'I could do with a holiday,' declared Felicity.

Dawlish grinned.

'Nothing doing. Ted, you, Robbie, and Fel had better stay here. I'll get Tony to keep me company on the Dorset trip.'

Beresford turned to Felicity with an expression of mock tragedy.

'It's no use arguing with him. He always gets his own way. If it were anyone else but Pat I'd get annoyed, but with Pat—'

Very soon afterwards, Dawlish and Grayling were driving towards the Great West Road in Dawlish's Lagonda.

He was thoughtful on the way down, and thankful that Tony did not show any particular desire to talk. They stopped in Andover for lunch, and said little of their purpose. Finishing his coffee with speed, Dawlish stood up.

'We'll be another hour and a half, I expect. Ready?'

'You don't give us much breathing space,' grinned Grayling. 'Yes, I'm ready. Who are you going to see first?'

'Mrs. Elizabeth Arthurson,' admitted Dawlish. 'She's first in alphabetical order.'

Grayling said curiously:

'By the way, why did you leave Ted and Robbie out of it?'

Dawlish shrugged.

'Robbie because I don't want him down here with me, yet. He's the pivot of the whole affair, and he'd be recognised too easily. To say the least of it, it's odd that these attempts should be made on him, and that Bateson should name three people whom he knows.'

'If you can see reason in it you're smarter than me,' admitted Grayling.

'There are glimmerings,' admitted Dawlish, 'but no more. As for Ted, I preferred him to stay near Felicity. Odd things might happen, and I don't think Robbie is enough on his own.'

They lapsed into silence.

It was turned three o'clock when they dove into Dorchester, and nearly twenty minutes past before Dawlish pulled the car up outside 9 Linden Drive. Few people were within sight, but as the car drew up a man left Number 9, glanced incuriously at the Lagonda as he passed.

Dawlish said swiftly:

'After him, Tony!'

Tony gaped. 'But what—'

'Shabby, vague-looking, hard to describe,' recited Dawlish. 'Beresford's man, or someone suspiciously like him. Off you go!'

Grayling tumbled out of the car and followed the shabby man, while Dawlish locked the doors and then approached the drive of the house, to make his first visit.

CHAPTER SIX

NOT A NICE SIGHT

Dawlish rang the bell and stood waiting for some minutes.

Walking up the drive he had seen that the house was an old one, its outline softened by creeper. There was ample evidence that it was the house of a person of taste and means.

There was no response to his ringing.

He lifted the heavy brass knocker, and brought it down with a resounding boom; but there was no reply. Frowning, Dawlish stepped back and looked up at the windows.

One at the top was open; all those on the ground floor were closed.

He rang again, then stepped to the side of the house. A large window revealed a pleasant room with a view through it to a further extension of the garden. There was a pond, some rose trees, and a hedge.

He turned in the other direction. A dining-room here, the sun glinting on highly polished furniture and brasses.

Dawlish experienced a queer sensation of suspense.

Had the man not come from the house he would have thought little of his failure to get a response. Obviously the owner could be out, and the fact that no one answered could be easily explained; domestic help was scarce, households which had been served by three or four servants before the war now managed with one. Or none, he reflected, and went round to the rear of the house.

The back door was standing open.

He stepped into a kitchen, glanced about him, and then called:

'Is anyone at home?'

Only the echoes of his voice answered him. He went through to the hall, and called again: waiting, he heard no sound excepting the vague noises which drifted in from the street.

He explored a morning-room, gay with chintzes and fresh flowers. Near a saddle-backed chair was a work-basket. Needles and cottons lay about, and a piece of half-finished embroidery lay on the chair arm.

Dawlish began to like it less and less.

He mounted the stairs, two at a time, and reached a square landing; five doors opened from it.

Dawlish looked into the nearest, finding it to be a bathroom. The second was a bedroom, a window framing a tall beech tree aflutter with birds.

There was quiet in the room—and something else.

Grim and motionless Dawlish looked down at the outstretched body. There was nothing he could do to help the woman; her throat was cut, and it was not a pleasant sight.

Dawlish did not know, but suspected that the body was that of Mrs. Elizabeth Arthurson.

She was a woman of perhaps sixty, the expression on her face that of frozen horror.

Dawlish swung about abruptly, and hurried downstairs; in

the morning-room he found a telephone. He lifted it, asked for the police station, and in a few seconds was speaking to the station sergeant.

He said clearly:

'I am speaking from Number 9 Linden Drive. A murder has been committed. My name is Dawlish, and I shall be here when your man arrives.'

He rang down without waiting for a reply, and retraced his steps.

Now that he had recovered from the first shock the sight of the murdered woman worried him less. He stepped to her, and knelt down.

Clutched in her right hand was a capacious handbag.

Dawlish opened it. There were the usual oddments which could have been in any woman's bag, but no letters and no papers. He straightened up, not quite decided on his best course. If he made a search he might make a lucky find, but in all probability the police would be able to do a much more comprehensive job in a shorter time. If they had received an order, or even a request, from London they would have to do what he wanted, but it was always advisable to keep them in a friendly frame of mind.

He stood looking about the room, both hands thrust deep in his pockets. Nothing attracted his attention until he saw marks on the window-sill. Bending over them he saw that there were fresh scratches on the paint.

He went downstairs, and into the garden.

A flower-bed close to the wall and beneath the bedroom window held footprints. Leaves had been trodden in, and the stems of a clump of flowers broken.

'There isn't much reconstruction needed here,' Dawlish decided aloud. 'The murderer came in through this window, and Mrs. Arthurson heard him and hurried upstairs. He'd be waiting behind the door when she entered.' His expression grew hard. 'I wonder what we *have* struck?' he asked of the silent garden.

The only sound apart from the birds, was the clatter of a lawn-mower not far away. The garden of Number 9 was walled, and above it grew high yew hedges; it was unlikely that anyone had seen the intruder, and in any case the police would check on that.

The sound of a car engine attracted his attention.

A moment later a man came into view.

'Polly!' breathed Dawlish. 'Robbie's digger!'

Approaching him with jaunty step was a man with white hair and absurdly rosy cheeks. He drew within a yard or two of Dawlish before stopping.

'Good afternoon, sir,' he said courteously. 'I do hope you're not going to tell me that Mrs. Arthurson is out.' He had a pleasant, rather high-pitched voice, and his eyes were a gentle, smiling blue. 'Seeing you come from the rear of the house I did wonder—of course, forgive me if I presume but—' He grew a little confused and broke off.

'That's perfectly all right, said Dawlish, knowing that the set expression on his face probably had much to do with the other's confusion. 'Do you know Mrs. Arthurson?'

'My dear sir, of course! Mrs. Arthurson and I are old and tried friends, I assure you. In fact I have called without sending word of my impending visit, knowing that I can always be sure of a welcome. But tell me, have you been trying to gain admittance?'

Dawlish hesitated.

He did not know how best to deal with the man, whom he was sure was Pollittzer. He liked the look of the old fellow, and it was easy to believe that the doctor was attached to Mrs. Arthurson.

If that were so the news of her death would be a great shock. There were other things; presumably Mrs. Arthurson had been killed because her name was on the list which Bateson had written; it followed that Pollittzer would be in like danger.

Dawlish said quietly:

'May I have your name, sir?'

'To be sure, I am Dr. Pollittzer. I—I do hope you will forgive me, but I am a little confused. Your name is—' He paused, invitingly.

'Dawlish,' said Dawlish.

Pollittzer showed neither surprise nor recognition.

'Ah,' he said, his eyes taking in the three pips on Dawlish's shoulder. 'I am glad to know you, Captain Dawlish. Have you knocked and obtained no reply?'

'Yes,' said Dawlish. 'I'm afraid I have some bad news for you, sir.'

'News?' echoed Pollittzer. 'Bad?'

'Dr. Pollittzer,' said Dawlish baldly, 'Mrs. Arthurson was murdered a short while ago.'

He saw the light fade slowly from the gentle blue eyes, the old, rosy face sag. Over Pollittzer there fell a sudden sadness. Sadness was the word rather than shock, thought Dawlish; *for Pollittzer showed no surprise.*

Nor did he question the statement. Instead:

'Poor, poor Elizabeth. God rest her soul.'

What might have transpired had they been left alone Dawlish did not know. The quiet of Linden Drive, which had something of the atmosphere of a cathedral close, was broken by noisy engines, then a squeaking of brakes. One car passed, and pulled up in front of the Lagonda, another stopped behind it. Three men climbed from both cars, and among them were two in uniform.

'Ah,' said Pollittzer softly. 'The police, of course, you have summoned them.' Sad and forlorn, he sank into a chair.

One of the men, tall and red-haired, approached smartly.

'Is your name Dawlish?' His voice was crisp.

'Yes,' said Dawlish. 'Inspector—'

'Superintendent Clay,' said the red-haired man briskly. 'It will save time and trouble, I think, if I tell you that I have had a request from London to offer you any assistance which you might need.' He smiled, as a proof of good-will rather than one of amusement. 'Where is Mrs. Arthurson? Have you seen her?'

'She is the victim,' said Dawlish quietly.

'Mrs. Arthurson!'

Dawlish explained briefly, but Clay did not need much telling. He gave swift orders to his men, then turned back to Dawlish.

'Are you coming up?'

Together they went up the stairs. 'You know the doctor, I take it?' Dawlish asked.

'Yes. Poor old boy,' said Clay. 'A great family friend. You've told him, I suppose?'

'He didn't seem surprised.'

Clay looked at him sharply, but Dawlish went on:

'If it's all right with you, I'd like to talk with him before you ask him questions. In fact I'd like you to forget that he didn't seem surprised, and accept my word for it that he arrived here after I'd discovered the murder. Tell me if I am trying you too far,' he added with a quick smile.

Clay frowned.

'We were asked to co-operate in every way, and are fully prepared to do so. Have you touched anything?'

'I looked in her handbag,' said Dawlish. 'No more than that.'

'Good,' said Clay. 'I was a little afraid—' He broke off. 'But

I think we understand each other. Is there anything you're looking for?'

Dawlish felt a quick satisfaction as he said:

'Yes, three things. Anything which might associate Mrs. Arthurson with a man named Bateson. That's one. Anything which might associate her with a man name Kohn, and thirdly, anything which might suggest that at any time during the past twelve months she had been frightened, or was seen to be apprehensive or nervous.'

'I'll find out what I can,' Clay promised.

Dawlish went downstairs.

Through the open front door he saw Tony Grayling walking towards the house at a fast rate, his face set.

CHAPTER SEVEN

'POLLY'

Grayling, ignoring the policeman standing in the porch, walked straight to Dawlish. Scenting trouble, Dawlish steered him gently into the dining-room and shut the door.

'Now what's the trouble?'

Grayling said sharply:

'This is a damnable business, Pat. I thought I could stomach most things, but there is a limit—' He paused, and then went on with somewhat of an effort: 'My customer had a car waiting near the High Street. I think he knew that I was after him for he went off at speed. There was an old lady walking across the road. *He ran her down.* Didn't even trouble to swerve.'

'And then what?' Dawlish asked mildly.

Grayling hesitated, eyeing his friend.

'You're an odd customer,' he said slowly. 'You can't be as callous as all that. I took the number of the car, of course, and gave it to the police. There's a call out for our man, but whether they'll get him is a different matter.'

'They'll keep him on the run, that's the main thing. Tony, go out and get the car turned, will you, we'll be off in a few minutes.'

Dawlish left Tony staring at him, then hurried into the lounge. Pollittzer was staring blindly out of the window.

'Dr. Pollittzer,' said Dawlish quietly. 'I would like to have a talk with you, for I think you might be able to help me. At the same time I have a journey to make. Where do you live?'

'At Poole,' said Pollittzer slowly.

'I am going in that direction. Will you come with me?'

Pollittzer raised his head and stared at him.

'That is a curious request,' he said softly.

'It's an urgent matter,' Dawlish assured him.

'You bewilder me,' said Pollittzer, and pressed a hand against his forehead. 'Poor Elizabeth, I can hardly believe it. I—yes, yes, Captain, I will come with you as you are so insistent. There is no purpose in my staying here now, no purpose at all. I would—I would like to see Elizabeth,' he added simply. 'Do you think it could be arranged?'

'I'll see what I can do.' Dawlish stepped past the constable stationed outside the bedroom door.

A photographer was packing up the tripod of his camera-outfit. Another man was walking about the room with a tin of powder in his hand, taking fingerprints. Clay was standing by the window, examining the scratches on it.

He looked up.

Dawlish saw Mrs. Arthurson's body on the bed. He was relieved to see that the wound was mercifully covered by a sheet.

Dawlish turned to Clay.

'I want to take Pollittzer away with me, if that's all right with you. Before he goes, he says he would like to see her. Is there any objection?'

Clay looked at the bed and then at Dawlish.

'What do you think?'

'It might be a good idea.' Dawlish paused. 'Meanwhile, you

should know that the man who probably killed her was coming away from here when I arrived. I'm not sure, but it's on the cards. A friend of mine followed him. The man escaped in a car, knocking down an old lady on the way. Your men in Dorchester have put a call out, and I expect that the roads are being watched.'

'Good,' said Clay, with a one-sided smile. 'You're not slow, Captain Dawlish.'

'Slow!' exclaimed Dawlish. 'If that was the man, I was twenty minutes too late, and if I'm not careful I'm going to be just too late for the next job.' He turned and hurried downstairs for Dr. Pollittzer.

The doctor stood looking at the dead woman for some time, his head bowed. Then he turned to Clay and Dawlish.

'Thank you, gentlemen. That was kind of you. I am at your service, Captain Dawlish.'

Outside, Dawlish opened the door for Pollittzer to climb into the tonneau, while directing Grayling to take the Wimborne road.

That done, he sat back and regarded Pollittzer in silence.

'Now, sir,' said the other at last, 'in what way do you imagine that I can help you?'

Dawlish said slowly:

'You surprised me, Doctor, with your first comment when I told you what had happened. As far as I can remember, you said, "Poor, poor Elizabeth. God rest her soul." You showed no astonishment whatever.'

Pollittzer answered quietly:

'When you reach my age, Captain Dawlish, and have seen death strike in so many unexpected places, you will learn that it takes a great deal to astonish one.'

'The reason was a little more than that, I think,' said Dawlish gently. 'I had the impression that you *expected* something of the kind to happen.'

Pollittzer said quietly: 'Elizabeth was not happy, Captain Dawlish. She lived under the shadow of death for a long time, and was both dismayed and afraid, although she covered her feelings bravely. Perhaps only I know how great was her courage.'

'I see,' said Dawlish.

After a pause, Pollittzer went on:

'I have told you that we were old and trusted friends, Captain Dawlish. I do not know whether she confided in others, but she did tell me that she was threatened with violence, and that she was frightened of being murdered. Unhappily, she withstood all my pressure to make her tell the authorities. I do not know why. I do not know why she was threatened. She kept that to herself, it was something she would not share even with me. She was a masterful woman; had you had the privilege of meeting her you would have learned that. So you can understand that I was not surprised, and that in a way I did expect it.'

'Ye-es,' Dawlish admitted.

Pollittzer glanced out of the window, speaking as they passed through a small village, of the countryside.

He talked on that subject for several minutes, then began to discuss the history of Dorset. Was Captain Dawlish acquainted with it? No? A pity, for in many ways it was the most interesting county in England.

Dawlish did not interrupt him.

It was possible that Pollittzer was talking to ease his grief, equally possible that he was riding his favourite hobby horse—Robbie Graham had suggested that—but it was also on the cards that he was deliberately evading the subject Dawlish had introduced. Dawlish could not make up his mind which was the more likely, but he brought the man back to the present by saying into a lull:

'When did Mrs. Arthurson's anxiety begin, Doctor?'

'Begin? I really don't know. She first told me of it some six months ago.'

'And she gave you no hint at all of the reason for the threats?'

'No, none,' Pollittzer assured him.

'I see. Do you know of anyone else who had been threatened?'

Pollittzer eyed him sharply.

'That is a somewhat strange question, Captain Dawlish.'

'This is a strange affair,' Dawlish pointed out. 'I would be glad of an answer, Doctor.'

'I know of no one,' said Pollitzer emphatically.

It looked to Dawlish as if Pollittzer were keeping something back; there was no reason to think that Bateson had misled them by putting the old man's name on the list. It was reasonable to suppose that Pollittzer *had* been threatened, and for the same cause as Mrs. Arthurson. If that were so, he had lied when he said that he knew nothing of the reason for the threats, or of their nature.

They were making good speed along a straight stretch of road with rolling country on either side of them. Soon afterwards a brick wall appeared on their right, and seemed to last for miles. They were nearing the end of it when two policemen at a road barrier raised their hands.

Tony's foot went down on the brakes.

Dawlish took a card from his wallet and handed it to the constable who had poked his head into the car. A glance told the man that Captain Patrick Dawlish had authority from Scotland Yard to travel where and when he liked, and he waved them on without further ado.

'You had little trouble there,' said Pollittzer with a gentle smile.

'There's trouble enough,' said Dawlish shortly. 'That was a barrier put up to try to stop Mrs. Arthurson's murderer.'

He spoke deliberately, watching the old man.

Pollittzer's eyes narrowed, and he exclaimed with some excitement:

'Her murderer! You know him?'

'I've seen him.'

'Why, that is astonishing,' said Pollittzer. 'In many ways, Captain Dawlish, I do not like our penal code, but the man who killed so good a woman deserves punishment—stern punishment.'

Pollittzer was either putting up a first-class act or else was really the rather rambling, good-natured little man he appeared to be, thought Dawlish. He reserved judgment.

'Do you know a place called The Lees, in Wimborne?'

Again Pollittzer appeared startled.

'The Lees? Is that where you are going?'

'It is.'

Pollittzer licked his lips.

'I—I do know the house, yes. It is on this side of the town. But I regret—I must insist—' He searched for words, and moistened his lips again. 'I must insist on being put down before we enter the grounds.'

'Why's that?' asked Dawlish.

'I hardly see the need for answering your question,' said Pollittzer stiffly. 'However, I will. The house belongs to an acquaintance of mine. I have sworn that I shall not step foot on his property again, and I will not do so. I must ask you to allow me to leave the car in a few minutes, Captain Dawlish.'

'There's no need for that,' said Dawlish promptly. 'I can get off there, and my friend can take you home. By the time I'm finished he'll be back.'

'There is no necessity for you to go to such trouble,' Pollittzer said quickly. 'If he will take me into Wimborne I can get a bus from there that almost passes my door. I should not dream of inconveniencing you further than that.'

'It's no trouble,' Dawlish assured him woodenly, 'no trouble at all.'

Pollittzer protested once again, then leaned forward to say to Tony:

Will you turn left here, please? The house you seek is along this road.'

In a few minutes the car drew up outside the white-painted gates of a house standing back on a slight rise. A Georgian house softened by creeper, it was not unlike 9 Linden Drive.

'This is as far as I shall go,' said Pollittzer firmly.

Dawlish asked no questions, but opened the door and climbed out. Grayling started to follow his example, but Dawlish said loudly:

'Take Dr. Pollittzer to Wimborne, Tony, will you? And then try to persuade him to let you run him right home. I'll be here for an hour,' he added, and then with his lips formed the words: 'Follow him.'

'Right-ho,' said Tony heartily.

Pollittzer was warm in his thanks. He was sorry that he could not do more to help Captain Dawlish, but it must be understood that he was suffering from the effects of a considerable shock. He was sure that the Captain appreciated his motives for not entering the drive of the Lees.

Dawlish watched the car out of sight.

There were so many curious things about Dr. Pollittzer that he wished he had more time to ponder them. He also wished that he had brought Ted and Robbie, and sent Felicity to friends. He needed more help than Tony's as things had turned out.

He wondered, too, whether he should have relied more on police assistance.

He shrugged his shoulders, and opened the drive gates.

Approaching the house, Dawlish was thinking that although he had come here on the spur of the moment, he would have been wrong to have waited. With Mrs. Arthurson murdered there was at least a chance that the shabby man would have a shot at Hennessy; and by the same reasoning, Pollittzer, too, was in danger.

'If,' mused Dawlish drily, 'he's not mixed up in it.'

He decided that it was much too early to jump to conclusions, and reached the porch.

It was uncannily like his visit to Mrs. Arthurson's. He rang the bell and stood back, half expecting to receive no answer.

Instead, footsteps echoed immediately.

A trim and youthful maid opened the door. Dawlish looked at her twice, for she was a pretty thing.

'Good evening. Is Mr. Hennessy in?'

'I'll find out, sir. What name, please?'

'Dawlish, Captain Dawlish.'

The maid stood aside to allow him to pass but was gone only a few seconds before returning.

'Mr. Hennessy is in,' she told him. 'Will you please come this way?'

Dawlish had come here because he had been afraid that Hennessy would be attacked, but nothing he saw suggested that anything untoward had, as yet, happened. He wondered whether he should have assumed that the murderer would be too busy trying to make his getaway to come here, then entered a study lined with books.

The man who rose from a high-backed chair at a desk was tall and grey. He was handsome, too, and smiling. He stepped towards the window to round his desk, and Dawlish, looking that way, saw a movement in the grounds.

He looked past Hennessy, whose expression changed abruptly, seeing a figure dart across a small lawn and lose himself in a shrubbery.

Dawlish felt quite sure that it was the shabby man of Linden Drive.

For a moment the man stopped by some bushes and peered up. Dawlish moved swiftly to one side of the window. The man outside stared again, and Dawlish saw that he was holding something in his right hand; he fancied that it was an automatic, and he unfastened the flap of his own holster as Hennessy said:

'What on earth is the meaning of this, sir?'

CHAPTER EIGHT

SHABBY LITTLE MAN

'At the moment I don't quite know' said Dawlish swiftly. 'Take my advice, and keep away from the window.'

They stood quite still for some seconds, and then Hennessy snapped:

'I insist on an explanation!'

He moved forward, making himself a clear target against the window.

Something hummed through the window, passing between Dawlish and Hennessy. There was a sharp sound as it struck the far wall. Then Dawlish fired, and the intruder dived into the shrubbery.

'Keep away from this window!' snapped Dawlish.

Peering out, he saw that a thick rope of ivy clung to the wall; it would enable him to climb down, but if he climbed he would be an easy target for the man outside. On the other hand, if he ran down the stairs to get into the garden, the man might easily get away.

Dawlish took the chance.

He saw Hennessy leaning against the desk, but did not see

the expression on the man's face. He put a foot over the window ledge and climbed out, holding his gun in one hand. He moved with astonishing agility, but there was an unpleasant feeling in the pit of his stomach.

With his feet finding purchase in the ivy and his free hand gripping the window ledge, he lowered himself as far as he could, and then let go.

As he dropped to the ground, he heard a sound above him. Pieces of dirt and chippings, as another bullet hit the wall, flew wide. He sprawled downwards, throwing himself flat.

Up again, he caught a glimpse of his quarry, further away now, and then the man disappeared.

Dawlish plunged forward.

If he hesitated he knew that he must lose his man, while in the confusion there was a fifty-fifty chance that the other's aim would be spoiled. Reaching the shrubbery, Dawlish saw that there was an orchard beyond. Again he caught a glimpse of his quarry, but before he could fire the man had vaulted a fence and disappeared into a thicket of scrub.

This led to an extensive wood, and when Dawlish reached it there was no trace of the intruder. A sharp voice spoke from behind him.

'Captain Dawlish!'

He turned to see Hennessy standing against the fence.

'How far does this wood stretch?'

'For a mile or more,' said Hennessy, startled into giving an answer. 'But—'

'I'll have to use your telephone,' interrupted Dawlish abruptly.

He vaulted the fence, wasting no time in asking Hennessy's permission. Approaching the house, he saw open french windows, and near them a telephone. He lifted it, and was asking the operator for the police, when Hennessy caught up with him.

Dawlish's first glimpse had shown the man's autocratic face, his fine eyes, and leonine head. On his greeting, Hennessy's voice had been mellow and pleasant, and he had smiled, now he was livid, his eyes glittering.

'Put that down at once!' His voice was thick with fury. 'I will not have this—this insolent trespass! Put that down, I tell you!'

Dawlish said into the telephone:

'I am speaking for the Dorchester police. A man for whom a call was circulated this afternoon has been seen in the woods at the back of The Lees, near Wimborne, the house of a Mr. Hennessy. Will you make what arrangements you can, please. My name is Dawlish.'

'Just a moment, sir.' The man who answered seemed excited.

'I haven't time,' said Dawlish. 'Pass the message on at once. It's urgent.'

He replaced the receiver, then stared into Hennessy's eyes.

Deliberately he waited, while Hennessy drew a deep breath, no wit less furious, and snapped:

'I shall report everything to the police! I saw you use that gun! What do you mean, breaking into my house and beginning such a murderous assault? I shall see that you suffer the severest penalty, I—'

Dawlish said: 'You were within a few inches of being killed, Mr. Hennessy.'

'Whatever you say cannot excuse such—*what* did you say?'

'I told you that you were within a few inches of being killed,' said Dawlish quietly. 'You're not particularly grateful, but I hope you will be.'

'Nonsense!'

'Please yourself.' Dawlish shrugged. 'I'm sorry I've messed up the flower-bed,' he added absently, 'but better that than another corpse.'

Hennessy backed a pace, staring at him in bewilderment. Despite the 'nonsense!' his manner changed, his anger was abating.

'Who *are* you?'

'It would be a good idea if we went inside and talked about this,' said Dawlish. 'May we go upstairs?'

Hennessy said dazedly:

'Er—yes. Yes, of course.'

Dawlish followed him up the stairs, passing the pretty maid who stood staring at them from the landing. Dawlish saw her wide-open eyes. Yet he was not altogether convinced that she was as frightened as she made out; in her expression as she turned away there was a calculating look.

Dawlish smoothed his hair thoughtfully.

Hennessy led the way into his study, stepping to the window and pulling it down. Not until then did he speak again.

'Now—now, sir, perhaps you will explain your astonishing behaviour. I cannot credit that there is any truth in what you have told me.'

'Nevertheless it is the truth,' said Dawlish drily. He turned to the wall opposite the window. At a point near a ledge on which stood several pieces of old china, was a single round mark. Dawlish pointed to it. 'That's where the bullet went in.'

'I can't believe it,' Hennessy repeated stubbornly.

He approached the spot and touched the hole. The bullet, a small one, was visible. Hennessy put a finger towards it, then drew it away hastily. When he turned round his face was pale.

'I cannot bear bloodshed or violence,' he said thickly. 'I cannot bear it, you need to understand that. And no one would wish to do me harm. That isn't possible.'

'Who do you think he tried to shoot?' demanded Dawlish drily.

'It could have been you,' said Hennessy.

Dawlish stared at him.

The other was an exceptionally good-looking man. In spite of his grey hair he looked little more than fifty-five. His eyes were grey, clear and unlined, his mouth well-shaped.

'Captain Dawlish,' he said stiffly. 'I insist on a fuller explanation.'

'I am trying to decide how to break it to you,' said Dawlish. 'Do you know a Mrs. Arthurson?'

Hennessy's lips tightened before he said:

'My private business is no concern of yours.'

'I think you may be wrong there,' said Dawlish gently. 'Mrs. Arthurson was murdered a few hours ago.'

Hennessy backed away, his hands raised. He might have been acting, but Dawlish was inclined to believe that it was the effect of a genuine shock. Hennessy's expression changed, too, defiance disappeared and something akin to horror replaced it.

'What—what are you saying!'

'That Mrs. Arthurson was murdered by the man whom I chased through your grounds,' said Dawlish. 'I saw the man leaving her house. I reached Mrs. Arthurson before she died, and she uttered a few words of some importance.'

Hennessy sat heavily in the chair behind the desk, and picked up a paper-weight. He played with it nervously.

'What did she say?'

'In effect, she said "save Hennessy",' declared Dawlish.

'Elizabeth said that! When she was—' Hennessy stopped abruptly, and his expression altered again. 'No, no, it isn't possible. I don't believe you! There is no reason at all why she should think of me at such a moment.' He dropped the paper-weight, and it struck the floor with a thud.

'You mean you don't want to believe it,' snapped Dawlish.

'Why should you say that?' muttered Hennessy.

'Oh, let's have finished with argument,' said Dawlish impatiently. 'The man attacked her, and I saw her before she died. I came here at once, and I was just in time, but only just in time, to save you. The warning came from Mrs. Arthurson, and it has proved necessary. If she had died before I saw her, you would be dead by now. Doesn't that make sense?'

Hennessy licked his lips.

'But—but it's incredible. No, no, I am not doubting your word, sir, but I cannot understand it, it is quite beyond me. Why should Elizabeth think that I might be in danger? Why should she think of me at all? We—we have not been on good terms for some time.'

'Aren't you forgetting another question?' demanded Dawlish.

'I don't follow you,' said Hennessy.

'Think it out,' said Dawlish, and paused. Then when the other remained silent he went on roughly: 'Isn't it strange that you're so damned anxious to say that there's no reason why she should talk of you that you forget to ask why she was killed?'

Hennessy stared at him, muscles in his cheeks and throat working. Then he pushed his chair back and stood up, speaking in a high-pitched and unnatural voice.

'I will not allow this! I don't know who you are, but I would not allow the police to come here and talk to me in this way. What are you trying to do?'

Dawlish said:

'To get at the truth. Hennessy, listen to me. I'm not a policeman. I knew that Mrs. Arthurson had been threatened, and I wanted to help her. She referred me to you in a way which was unmistakable. She told me enough for me to know that you also had been threatened. As a result I came here, and saved your life, and as payment I want to know who threatened you, and why. I don't care a damn what guilty secret you're hiding. I'm not the police, but I want results and I'm going to get them. I mean to find out why you and Mrs. Arthurson were threatened, and whether you know of anyone else who might have been.'

'You—you're talking nonsense,' Hennessy insisted thinly. 'I am completely at a loss.'

'If I'd been ten minutes later you would have been dead,' Dawlish repeated roughly. 'Doesn't that mean anything to you?'

'No, no!' cried Hennessy. 'I don't believe you. The attack was against you! I've never been threatened in my life, I can't be in danger!'

Dawlish said slowly:

'So you're going to keep that up.'

'Of course I am, it's the truth!'

Dawlish shrugged, and half turned.

'All right, please yourself. But it's my turn now. I don't believe you. I shall have you watched and followed wherever you go. Sooner or later I'll find out what's been happening to you, and just what you know.'

'Dawlish!'

'You heard me,' rasped Dawlish, stepping towards the door.

'Dawlish!' Hennessy rounded the desk and approached him, a hand outstretched. Dawlish turned to see his face damp with perspiration, and his lips unsteady. 'Dawlish, what right have you to talk like this?'

'You'll find that out.'

'I—I insist on knowing now!'

Dawlish smiled without humour.

'Your insisting isn't going to do you much good,' he said sardonically. 'But I'll tell you that I've all the authority I need, and no appeal to the police will help you. Good-day.'

He opened the door, walking swiftly and deliberately. There was a flurry of movement, and as he reached the hall Hennessy caught up with him.

A door closed sharply, but no one was in sight.

'Dawlish, don't go,' said Hennessy urgently. 'I—I hardly know what to say. There is some grievous misunderstanding. Elizabeth made a grave mistake, and I can't understand it. I'm sure that she meant someone else; she couldn't have meant me. Why, it's absurd! Why should I be threatened?'

'Why have you been?' demanded Dawlish, and opened the front door.

Hennessy did not follow him again.

Dawlish stood for some seconds on the porch.

A man turned into the drive and walked quickly towards the house. Dawlish waited until the other came nearer. The newcomer, an athletic-looking, middle-aged man, drew up in front of Dawlish.

'Are you Mr. Dawlish?' He spoke quietly.

'That's right.'

'You telephoned the police station,' said the other. 'I am Inspector Medway of the Dorset C.I.D. The woods have been surrounded and are being searched, although there has been plenty of time for your man to get away.'

'That's what's worrying me,' admitted Dawlish. 'Inspector, can you spare a good man for a few hours?'

'Yes,' said Medway promptly.

'Then,' said Dawlish quietly, 'I would like Mr. Hennessy watched. It's possible that his life is in danger, I think he was attacked by the man I've seen. Mr. Hennessy doesn't take kindly to the idea, but until I can send someone to look after him I'd like to feel that you are watching out for trouble.'

'I'll arrange that,' Medway assured him. 'We've had

instructions from the Home Office to afford you all the help we can, and we'll do it. Is there anything else?'

'Ye-es. Hennessy was threatened some time ago. I don't know why, and I want to find out. Also I'd like to know just when it happened, and whether you had reports of anything at the time.'

Medway frowned and looked past Dawlish to the house.

'That's not so easy,' he said. 'Hennessy isn't popular about here, and I know that some of the wilder spirits have made his life uncomfortable. He's a pacifist with emphatic views, and he doesn't hesitate to express them. We've been called several times to deal with threats put over by anonymous letters and by telephone. That isn't the kind of thing you mean, is it?'

'No,' said Dawlish. 'Has he ever seemed particularly frightened?'

'Frightened, anyhow,' admitted Medway. 'I don't think there's anything serious in these threats, but they've got on his nerves and I suppose that's understandable enough.'

'Ye-es,' said Dawlish slowly. 'It complicates things, too, but you might check carefully on the letters and incidents which you haven't been able to trace.'

'I'll do that.'

The two men looked up as a car turned into the drive. Dawlish recognised his Lagonda, with Grayling at the wheel.

'Ah. My car's come back.' Tony drew up with a scowl:

'This definitely isn't my day. He got away.'

'It certainly isn't,' agreed Dawlish. 'How did it happen?'

'He wouldn't let me drive him home,' said Grayling, 'and said there was a bus waiting in the Square. He was so insistent about it that I let him go. I don't know whether it was arranged or not, but he slipped away somewhere. He wasn't on the bus, anyhow.'

Dawlish rubbed the side of his nose and looked at Medway. 'Inspector, there is something else after all. Have a call put out for Dr. Pollittzer, of Poole, will you? And if you find him, treat him exactly in the same way as Hennessy.'

The Inspector drew a sharp breath, staring at him in obvious astonishment.

Before Medway could speak, the door of the house opened and a girl stepped out. Dawlish recognised the maid. She was dressed in outdoor clothes that were both expensive and in good taste. Dawlish looked after her uncertainly, for she did not look like a maid on her afternoon off.

He turned back to Medway.

'Well?'

Medway said: 'This is beyond me. I—' He drew a deep breath, and then added sharply: 'Dr. Pollittzer died this afternoon. He collapsed in the street, and was dead before he reached hospital.'

CHAPTER NINE

ENCOUNTER ON THE ROAD

Dawlish stared into the Inspector's face for some seconds. Tony uttered a sharp exclamation, and then silence fell about them.

Dawlish said at last:

'I think I brought him from Dorchester not two hours ago, Medway. Would Clay, of Dorchester, know him?'

'Yes, of course,' said Medway.

'Then Clay thought it was Pollittzer.'

Medway ran a hand over his head, and then said practically:

'Give me the approximate time you saw him and left him, will you? I'll make arrangements about Hennessy, and then go over to Poole and find out what I can. Will you be staying in the district over night?'

'I'm not sure yet. I'll phone you later.'

'Thanks.' Medway left them, taking a short cut through trees and shrubs. Dawlish and Grayling eyed one another without expression, then Grayling said explosively:

'What *is* this?'

'One thing sticks out a mile,' said Dawlish thoughtfully. 'We didn't have the real Pollittzer. That face was always too good to be true. False beard and hair, obviously. A beak of a nose, too. I wish to heaven I'd tweaked it!'

'But—' began Grayling bewilderedly.

'Where are the buts?' demanded Dawlish. 'You saw him in Wimborne, didn't you? He actually boarded the bus.'

'Ye-es.'

'You didn't see him get off?'

'Now what are you getting at?' demanded Grayling with a touch of irritation. 'He could have slipped off while I was turning the car. I took it for granted that he did, anyhow. I didn't ask anyone else if they'd seen him, I thought it would be too obvious.'

'It would have been,' Dawlish admitted. 'What did you do?'

'I went to the bus, and looked upstairs and down,' said Grayling.

'The probability is that you saw him,' said Dawlish. 'Two minutes would probably be ample for the gentleman to take off the wig and the whatnots.'

Grayling drew a deep breath.

'Oh my lord! There was a little customer, bald-headed except for a fringe of grey hair. He would have fitted the part.' Grayling paused, and then said slowly: 'Pat, I'm not the slightest use to you. This is the third time I've bungled a job.'

Dawlish smiled good-humouredly.

'Don't let that worry you. I've done nothing but bungle since the affair started. The incidentals aren't important, and we've travelled a long way since last night.' He paused, and then added: 'Is anyone watching us from the house? Don't look up too obviously.'

Grayling glanced away, as if bored and inattentive at what was being said.

'There's a man behind the curtains at one of the windows.'

'Ha. So Hennessy's still very curious,' commented Dawlish.

He climbed into the car, taking the wheel. Grayling joined

him. Dawlish drove slowly along the drive, turning left, towards Wimborne, he changed gear and was about to accelerate when a girl appeared from the side of the road.

It was Hennessy's maid, standing with an arm upraised. There was nothing surprising in that, for a dozen times on the drive to Dorchester they had passed people who wanted a lift.

Dawlish braked, and Grayling wound down his window.

'I wonder if you would mind giving me a lift?' asked the maid quietly. 'I'm going into Wimborne.'

With a murmured assent Grayling leaned over and opened the rear door. The girl climbed in.

Dawlish could see her in the driving mirror. She puzzled him.

He remembered the hurried movements in the house when he had left Hennessy's room, and the door which had closed.

Approaching cross roads at the outskirts of the town, Dawlish slowed down and turned his head.

'Do I go straight on?' he asked.

'For the Square, yes.'

'Will that suit you?' he asked again.

'Yes, it's where my bus starts for Bournemouth.'

'Bournemouth?' said Dawlish with a smile. 'That's where we're going.'

The girl settled back in her seat. Then: 'I'd be very grateful if you'd take me all the way.'

'Of course,' said Dawlish. He grew talkative.

The girl chatted back in a pleasant, cultured voice, while Dawlish grew even more curious.

In something over twenty minutes they were driving into the centre of Bournemouth, and he asked her where he should drop her.

'Anywhere here,' she said.

'We're looking for a hotel,' said Dawlish, 'do you know of one?'

'The Palace Court should suit you,' he was told. 'You can't miss it. It's right opposite the Pavilion.'

Dawlish braked the car, and jumped out to open the door.

The girl smiled at him and thanked him, then walked unself-consciously away, mingling with the crowd.

Dawlish looked at Grayling with a thoughtful smile.

'I'm curious about that young woman. She's Hennessy's maid. Did she strike you that way?'

'His *maid*?' echoed Grayling.

'Yes. Do you wonder that I'm curious?'

'Then why the deuce aren't you following her?' demanded Grayling energetically.

Dawlish chuckled.

'If she's worth following, it's worth hiding suspicions at the moment, Tony. We'll let her have a free run for a bit. Hennessy's place is going to be watched, and it'll be just as well if she's watched too, without knowing it.'

He took the wheel again, and in a few minutes had booked in at the Palace Court Hotel.

'Will you be wanting dinner, sir?'

'That's an idea,' said Dawlish. He glanced at his watch. 'Half past eight, by George. Can you get us a meal in about an hour's time?'

'Yes, I'll arrange that,' the receptionist promised.

The registration forms were filled in and signed, and Dawlish stepped into the foyer. Grayling eyed him in some exasperation.

'Why couldn't we eat straight away? We haven't had any tea, and I'm ravenous.'

'We've another appointment,' Dawlish told him.

'Where?'

'An address in Westbourne,' said Dawlish. 'It's only just struck me that Westbourne's a suburb of Bournemouth. The venue of this show certainly seems to be in this part of the world.' He laid a hand on Tony's shoulder, and chuckled. 'Sorry old man. The first man on Bateson's list was a Mr. James Rennett, of 18a The Grove, Westbourne.'

He was thinking of all that had happened since he had reached Dorchester. It was difficult to get it in the right perspective, too many different things had happened. When he concentrated for a few minutes on Pollittzer, or the man who pretended to be Pollittzer, he found himself thinking of Hennessy, and then of Hennessy's maid.

As he drove the car he was telling himself that he had made at least one fatal error. It was too late to make amends thoroughly, since Mrs. Arthurson was dead.

He might have saved her.

It was not altogether his fault. Whitehead had virtually approved his approach to the case. But now it seemed obvious that he should not have kept the Dorset addresses so much to himself. Had he asked the Dorset police to keep an eye on Mrs. Arthurson, Pollittzer and Hennessy, he might have saved the first two.

He had assumed that the genuine Pollittzer was dead, and that he and Clay had been deceived. A corrollary to the assumption was that Pollittzer had been murdered. That he had collapsed in a crowded street suggested the possibility of a drug.

The Grove proved to be a wide, tree-lined avenue, with large houses on either side. 18a, was a pseudo-Elizabethan residence, surrounded by pines and beech trees. It looked pleasant enough, even picturesque, and Dawlish drove slowly past it.

He pulled the Lagonda up fifty yards along the road, and they walked back. Dawlish was pondering over a means of approach to Rennett but knew that whatever he decided might have to be discarded. Plans, in his experience, were so often rudely shattered that impromptu arrangements were more satisfactory.

'I suppose I am to wait outside,' said Grayling, plaintively.

Dawlish grinned sympathetically.

'I don't see why, this time. There's no one else in this part of the world, as far as I know, and I've a feeling that the shabby cove won't turn up again just yet.'

'Your feelings make me uncomfortable,' declared Grayling. 'There's no sense in them.'

'I've never met anyone who doesn't agree with you,' admitted Dawlish. 'Anyhow, I'll give you three to one that we don't see the little devil again tonight.' Half-way up the drive, he added: 'Well, put it this way, Tony, he's committed one murder, or we're assuming that he has, and tried another. The hue-and-cry after him is getting stronger, and sooner or later he'll have to lay low. If he's got any sense at all it'll be sooner. What's more, the directing intelligence behind this business isn't going to allow one man, the same man, to do everything. If Rennett is in danger, it's from someone we haven't met yet.'

'I suppose that is reasonable,' admitted Grayling.

They reached the porch, and Dawlish pressed the bell.

Some seconds passed before there was any response, and then the sound of a bolt being pulled back came to them.

The door opened.

Dawlish opened his lips, then kept them that way. Grayling uttered a sharp exclamation, while the girl standing at the door eyed them without expression. She looked from one to the other, and then stood aside.

'Won't you come in?' she asked.

'Er—thanks,' said Dawlish.

He stepped past her into a hall, and Grayling followed. The girl closed the door and then regarded them steadily, a glimmer of a smile in her eyes.

She was Hennessy's maid.

CHAPTER TEN

MR. RENNETT DISCOURSES

Dawlish recovered himself quickly.

'It's a pity we didn't know you were coming,' he said drily. 'We could have brought you right to the door.'

'You've already been good enough,' she answered gravely. 'I assume that you want to see Mr. Rennett?'

'That's right,' said Dawlish.

'He won't keep you long,' said the girl. She led the way to a lounge, then left the room closing the door behind her.

Dawlish and Grayling eyed one another in startled silence before Grayling exclaimed:

'Well, I'm damned!'

'Ye-es,' said Dawlish slowly. 'Heaven knows we should have thought of it, but I didn't have a glimmering of an idea. She's a self-possessed young woman.'

'What's she up to?' demanded Grayling.

'We'll find out,' Dawlish assured him.

Several minutes passed before the girl reappeared. With a brief comment she led them upstairs, pausing before one of the doors.

'Mr. Rennett asks me to apologise for him,' she said. 'He's been confined to his bed for several days.'

She tapped on the door, then opened it.

In a large, airy room a man was sitting up in bed, propped with pillows. He was smoking a pipe.

No one else could have looked less like an invalid than Mr. James Rennett.

He had a weather-beaten face, bright brown eyes, and a humorous mouth. He smiled up at them crookedly, took his pipe from his lips and waved it towards some chairs standing on the far side of the bed, then:

'Good evening, gentlemen. Do sit down. Now which of you young gentlemen is Captain Dawlish?'

'I am,' said Dawlish quietly.

'I'm very interested to meet you,' said Rennett, and chuckled. 'Vi's told me what happened at The Lees. You've wasted a lot of time in my opinion. Hennessy's no good to anyone. He'd be better dead.' He turned to the girl. 'Vi, I think I'd better introduce you. This is Captain Dawlish, and—'

'Captain Grayling,' said Dawlish.

'Miss Elvira Templeton, my niece. Sit down, Vi, you're in this.'

The girl drew up another chair, and sat opposite the visitors.

'Well, Captain Dawlish,' said Rennett heartily, 'you wanted to see me. What about?'

Dawlish said:

'I'm not sure.'

'Not sure be damned!' snapped Rennett, his mood changing abruptly. 'I call a spade a spade, and I expect others to do the same. Out with it.'

Dawlish smiled. 'Yet the truth still remains, that I'm not sure why I came to see you.'

Rennett scowled. 'That's nonsense.'

'Is it?' asked Dawlish. 'I had your name as a friend of Mrs. Arthurson and an acquaintance of Hennessy's. I came because I thought you might be able to tell me something about them, but it wasn't a clear-cut idea. I suppose I just wanted to see you.'

'Humph. A general weigh-me-up, is that it?'

'You could call it that.'

Rennett scowled again.

'What's that but damned evasion?'

'That's partly your fault, and partly Miss Templeton's.' Dawlish assured him. 'I'm still recovering from surprise.'

'Surprise, eh?' Rennett chuckled. 'That's understandable enough. I said to Vi, if those two hearties come along here after they've left you, they'll get a shock they didn't expect.'

'Ye-es,' said Dawlish. 'Why should you think it possible that we should come?'

Rennett fiddled with his pipe.

'Thereby hangs a tale, young fellow, and I'm going to tell it to you. But I'm not going to start until I've had the truth out of you. Don't try to fill me up with a lot of twaddle about knowing I was an acquaintance of Mrs. Arthurson and Hennessy. I know them, yes, but you had something stronger than that. You might lie to Hennessy and get away with it, but you can't to me. Now then, why did you come?'

Dawlish eyed him evenly.

Quick thinking was called for, pros and cons had to be weighed before he committed himself. Watching the other's keen, shrewd eyes, he decided that it would be difficult to lie convincingly to Rennett, but that was no argument for telling all he knew.

How much danger would there be in telling the truth?

He was thinking, too, that Rennett's protestations of being a blunt and honest man might be a bluff designed to draw him out.

'Well, come on,' said Rennett testily. 'You don't need all day to make up your mind.'

Dawlish smiled.

'Mr. Rennett, your name was on a list of names and addresses which came by chance into my possession. So was Hennessy's, and Mrs. Arthurson's. I had reason to believe that the names and addresses were of interest to an organisation—'

'Organisation!' exclaimed Rennett explosively. 'If you mean gang, say gang. I've never used five syllables where one will do, and I'm not going to start now. Go on.'

Dawlish said gently:

'You know, Mr. Rennett, I'm not sure that I like your manner.'

'You don't *what*?' roared Rennett.

'Like your manner,' replied Dawlish.

There was a brief but tense silence; and then Rennett burst into explosive laughter.

'Well, well. I don't know that I like yours. Still, I'm curious. So you can get on with your fairy story. I haven't spent a lifetime at sea without hearing some tall ones!'

'Ah yes,' said Dawlish equably. 'I think the names and addresses are of importance to an organisation in which the police and other authorities are interested. I want to find out what I can about these people, and the names and addresses offer a prospect of results. I visited Mrs. Arthurson first; she was murdered before I arrived.'

Rennett nodded: 'I know, yes.'

'How do you know?' asked Dawlish.

'Vi told me,' said Rennett promptly. 'She heard you talking. That's what she's at Hennessy's for.' He grinned again, as if enjoying a secret joke. 'Then you went to Hennessy, and Vi tells me you saved him from going the same way as Beth. You know what I think about that. Then what?'

'I came here,' said Dawlish.

'Humph,' said Rennett. 'I'm beginning to see what you mean by saying that you don't know why you came here. Plenty of reasons, none of them clear-cut. Is that right?'

'That's right.'

'Well, I'm taking your word for it,' said Rennett. 'I don't know why *you're* interested, personally.'

Dawlish said: 'That's easy.'

Rennett flashed: Intelligence service?'

'What makes you think so?'

Rennett said shrewdly: 'Vi said the police were very anxious to help you.'

'Miss Templeton has good ears,' said Dawlish coldly. 'Actually I have friends at Scotland Yard, and I took my problem to them. It's a personal one. A friend of mine was attacked, and I tried to find out why. In the process of the inquiries I discovered the list. My friend's name was on it.'

'I see,' said Rennett. 'And then the police just said: "Go and do what you like"? That's a fine yarn,' he added jeeringly. 'Can't you think up a better one?'

It was then that the girl interrupted.

'You've been out of England a long time, Uncle. If you'd been here you would have read that Captain Dawlish has been in the headlines quite often. One of the papers calls him a private investigator.'

'No!' exclaimed Rennett, peering at Dawlish. 'What, a 'tec!'

There was a moment of silence. Then Dawlish pushed his chair back and stood up.

He was quite sure that Rennett was trying to anger him. That the girl had joined in the baiting widened the issue, and he did not propose to let either of them get away with it.

'Now supposing we get down to business?' he suggested

pleasantly. 'I can't make you tell me anything, Mr. Rennett, but I needn't waste my time, as I am doing at the moment.'

Rennett glared.

'You're a damned offensive fellow.'

'I'm not going to argue about that,' said Dawlish. 'Have you anything to say to me, or haven't you?'

He expected an outburst; instead, Rennett said gruffly:

'Come on, sit down. You're no fool, that's what I wanted to be sure about. You want to know why I'm interested in Hennessy, don't you?'

'I do.'

'All right, here you are. I've known him a long time. Don't like the fellow, and never have. I always told Beth Arthurson that she was crazy to have anything to do with him, but you can never advise a woman. That's one thing. Another—I've been abroad a long time. Did a Hong Kong-Penang run for more years than I like to remember. I got out by the skin of my teeth before the Japs came. I came back home, and got another ship. Torpedoed, and that knocked my legs about a bit. Half my time I'm chained to this damned bed, if I weren't I'd get around a darned sight quicker than you do.'

'I can guess you'd try,' said Dawlish.

'Humph!' grunted Rennett. 'All right, smarty, listen to this. I was in Singapore when I saw Hennessy. Damned odd thing happened—he ignored me. Walked straight past me. What would you think, Dawlish, if you met a man from your home town ten thousand miles away, and he walked past you?'

'Before you go on,' said Dawlish, 'did you ever live nearer to Hennessy than you do now?'

'Yes. I was at Wimborne before I left the country for the East,' Rennett drew on his pipe. 'Let me tell you, I kept a rod in pickle for Hennessy. I knew he'd come off a P. & O. ship, you understand, and I made it my business to run across her skipper at Raffles Hotel. I wanted to know how he got on with Hennessy.'

Dawlish said quietly:

'And I suppose you found he was travelling under an assumed name?'

Rennett nodded.

'You're damned right, he was. It might seem obvious to you, but it didn't to me. This was fifteen months ago. I wasn't blind to what was happening. I've known the Japs half of my life, and I knew what they were after. I didn't link that up with Hennessy,' added Rennett, 'but believe me I was curious. So I asked a few questions. He was travelling under the name of Bonnington, and was supposed to be on a cruise for his health. In point of fact he was in contact with a lot of oil people. Then I left Singapore. I didn't forget about him, and when I wrote to Vi I told her what had happened. Now believe it or not, Dawlish, when she got my letter Hennessy was back in England.'

'The letter came by air mail, and he flew back,' said Dawlish. 'That's easy.'

'Easy, is it?' growled Rennett. 'He had booked a passage on the ship, so why did he change his mind?' Rennett paused, and stared into Dawlish's eyes. 'Now you're asking yourself what else I did, and saying that I'm an interfering old know-all. That's as maybe. I didn't forget it, and nor did Vi.'

'Just a minute,' said Dawlish. 'Didn't Hennessy know your niece?'

'He'd known her as a schoolgirl, that's all. They weren't really acquainted. Well, I'll cut it short, Dawlish. I came back not long afterwards, and damn me if the first thing I got was a telephone call telling me not to interest myself in other people's business! No name, but you can see where my mind turned. Hennessy, I decided, and he was up to no good. Then someone tried to push me over the cliff—you know the cliffs here?'

'Slightly,' said Dawlish.

'They're dangerous at night. There was a black-out. I was having a stroll, and someone pushed me. He ran off as soon as I'd recovered, but it wasn't a picnic. Then I had one or two letters saying much the same as the telephone call. I don't mind telling you, Dawlish, that I nearly went over to see the old buzzard. I would have done if Vi hadn't stopped me. Then I had to go into hospital for a couple of months. When I came out I was looking at the papers, and what did I see? Why, Hennessy wanted a maid!

'A maid,' repeated Rennett with a wide grin. 'I looked at Vi, and she looked at me, and then I nearly died of laughing. Just the chance, said I. You can find out what he's up to, and let me know.'

'So you went straight to Hennessy and got the job?' asked Dawlish, turning to Elvira.

She nodded.

'How long ago was that?'

'Three weeks,' Elvira looked at her uncle. 'I don't think we're being believed,' she added quietly.

Rennett glared. 'Why the devil not? Let me tell you, Dawlish, that she's learned a lot of very interesting things about Hennessy. *Very* interesting things. Eh, Vi?'

Suddenly there came a sound from downstairs.

Elvira started to her feet in quick alarm.

'Did you hear that?' She spoke sharply. 'There shouldn't be anyone else in the house.'

Into the pause which followed there came another sound, and then a silence broken only by their breathing.

CHAPTER ELEVEN

STRANGE VISITOR

Dawlish and Grayling moved resolutely to the door. Dawlish's hand had already touched it when it swung open.

A man stood there, and in his hand was a gun. He was followed by a second man, short and swift-moving. He, too, was armed. He covered the others, while the man in the doorway, tall, and black-clad, stared at Dawlish without speaking.

There was about him a peculiar stillness. It affected his face as well as his body. Even when he moved it was stiffly, as if he was worked by mechanism.

Rennett let out a bellow of rage.

'What the hell is this?'

Hitching himself high on his pillows he stretched to the bedside table, and pulled at a drawer.

The smaller man moved swiftly across the room, turning his gun in his hand. He banged the drawer shut, then, raising his arm, cracked the butt of his automatic against Rennett's temple.

Rennett gasped and dropped back on the pillows.

The man struck him again, and Elvira cried:

'Stop him, stop him! You cowards!' She sprang forward, but

Tony caught, and held her. With Rennett slumped down in the pillows, a trickle of blood coming from his injured temple, the man seemed satisfied. He was not much more than four feet tall, but he was broad and looked powerful.

'That'll teach the rest of yer,' he said harshly. 'Do's yer told.'

'One day,' said Dawlish evenly, 'you'll be sorry about that.' He turned to the man in black. 'What do you want?' he demanded.

In the better light the uncanny impression which the man had created on first sight was heightened. His face was pallid—but it was not a natural pallor. Dawlish decided that the effect was caused by some kind of theatrical make-up.

He said: 'I came to see you, Dawlish.'

The words were uttered on a monotonous level, neither high nor low. He stood quite still with his gun covering Dawlish, as if waiting for some response. Dawlish said drily:

'Well, here I am.'

The man in black said: 'I think it will not be necessary to warn you that you must stand still. I will shoot at the first sign of movement.'

Dawlish glanced at Grayling, and shrugged.

'What do you want?'

There was no hint of expression on the pale face or in the shadowy eyes. Behind Dawlish, Elvira was bending over her uncle, the short man watching her closely. Dawlish felt that he would need little, if any, encouragement to use his gun.

The situation would have been less unnerving had there been anything normal about the man in black. The only movement of his face was when he spoke; he did not seem to be breathing. Though Dawlish realised that the face was plastered over to create a weird impression of immobility and at the same time to form an effective disguise, it did nothing to ease the tension.

'I have told you,' said the man in black. 'I came to see you,

Dawlish. You have visited a number of places today. You appear to be curious.'

Dawlish forced a smile.

'Curious?' he said, 'who says I'm curious?'

'You give that impression,' the other answered.

'Well, look at the impression you're trying to create,' said Dawlish. 'You aren't succeeding, but you're trying damned hard. I mean, that illustrates the unreliability of impressions, doesn't it?'

'Be quiet,' said the man softly.

'Why, I'm just warming up,' said Dawlish. 'Anyhow, I thought you were interested in my motives.'

Tony shot him a quick sideways glance. To Tony, that day had been a revelation; he had seen Dawlish at work, had seen the speed with which he acted, and was profoundly impressed.

'I told you to be quiet,' repeated the man in black.

'All right, all right,' said Dawlish testily. 'One last word, isn't that what they say in these circumstances? I'm not curious because I know practically everything. And I am not alone.'

He smiled.

'You think you do,' said the man in black.

'Please yourself,' said Dawlish.

There was a short silence, and the man in black said slowly:

'Dawlish, I first heard of you after Bateson's clumsy effort to kill Graham. It was even more clumsy than it appeared to you, because Bateson attempted to kill the wrong man. I will not go further into that, but it will illustrate the degree of your good fortune. But for that serious error, you would have known nothing whatever. As it is—'

'No, I can't let that pass,' interrupted Dawlish.

'What do you mean?' snapped the other.

It was the first time his calm had broken.

There was a hint of a smile in Dawlish's eyes.

'I should have known as much,' said Dawlish, 'even without Bateson's ineptitudes.'

The man in black took a step forward, and said very softly:

'You are lying.'

Dawlish said easily: 'Now look here, we aren't getting anywhere by talking in circles. If you don't want to hear the truth, why keep up the conversation? I realise that it must be unpleasant for you to learn that we've been looking for you for a long time, but there it is. We haven't yet discovered just why you came here,' he added easily. 'Are you going to tell us?'

'I came to talk to you,' said the man in black. 'I came to find what had inspired your interest, and I came to warn you. I do not know who you are, and I do not greatly care. You may or may not be connected with the authorities. It is not a matter of great importance. But you will not succeed in finding out my business. Rather than allow that, I shall kill you. But,' went on the man in black, 'I have no wish to do that, Dawlish.'

Dawlish said easily: 'Strange. I'd certainly gathered the impression that you and your friends were a little careless about corpses.'

'That is a different matter. Those who have died are useless, while you are a useful man, playing a part in this war. The death of the others does not matter; your death might matter a great deal. You are a man of parts, and I judge that you are no fool. Take my advice and devote your energies to your country's cause. Remember that this is private vengeance and leave it to the police. Do you understand me?'

Dawlish said: 'Oh yes, I understand you.'

'I am glad. Be warned that any of your friends who ignore this advice and take a part in operations against me will be treated ruthlessly.' He paused, then looked at Elvira: 'So will you, and your uncle. You will not return to Hennessy. He has been told who you are.'

The man in black edged towards the door, followed by his companion.

'Remember,' he said.

As they drew out of sight the lock clicked. Dawlish snatched his gun from his holster and approached it from one direction, Tony from the other.

There was the sound of heavy footsteps outside, the creaking of stairs. A downstair door slammed.

Elvira was nearer the window than either of the men, and she reached it in a few quick strides, pulling back the curtains. There was no sign of movement, no indication that the two men had left the house that way.

'What are you going to do?' she demanded.

Dawlish shrugged. 'What can we do? They've bested us this time. We haven't a chance of catching them.'

'You can try!' flashed the girl.

'Why waste the effort?' asked Dawlish. 'Why not just be satisfied that we're alive? That's something I didn't expect.' He was smiling a little, but the expression in his eyes was bleak. 'We should have been dead, you know, he's no humanitarian.'

The girl drew a deep breath.

'Don't stand there talking nonsense, go after them! It's madness! You can't do nothing!'

'Yes, I can,' said Dawlish languidly. 'My sweet, you can't have everything you own way. Tony and I are handling this, and Tony's in full agreement.' He winked at his friend. 'All we wanted to do was to make them think we were after them, even if we'd seen them in the garden a couple of wild shots would have been enough for that.'

Elvira said hotly: 'You're crazy!'

'No, just being fair,' said Dawlish. 'They let us stay alive, so for the time being we'll let them do the same.' He stepped to the bed, and frowned down on Rennett. 'Ought you to get a doctor?'

'A—a doctor,' gasped Elvira in a strangled voice. 'Why, if he'd been conscious he would have shown you how to handle them, he would have had the police here by now, the whole street would have been roused!'

'That's just what we didn't want,' said Dawlish gently. 'Don't get hysterical, Elvira. What about that doctor?'

'If you say "that doctor" again, I'll scream! He doesn't need a doctor, he'll be all right soon. I can dress the wound myself.' She glared at him angrily, and then hurried out of the room.

There followed the clatter of a bowl, and water running swiftly from a tap.

Grayling looked helplessly at Dawlish.

'You know, Pat,' he said, 'I'm inclined to agree with her.'

Dawlish said moodily:

'You haven't tried to sort it out, that's the trouble. What do you suppose that visit was for?'

'I'm damned if I know,' said Tony.

'Think,' urged Dawlish. 'He could have killed us. We might have done some damage to him, but he had the upper hand from the start and he's no fool. He talked a lot of tripe, and then went off. The only damage was to Rennett, and that was incidental. Why did he come?'

'He didn't just come to talk,' said Grayling slowly.

'You're wrong,' said Dawlish. 'That's exactly what he came for. He came—' He watched the door open, and the girl enter with a bowl of water and a towel slung over her arm. He did not pause, but repeated: 'He came because he wanted to create an impression, and to tell us something. Out of those hollow menaces two things emerged. One, that Bateson was after the wrong man. Two, that it's a matter of private vengeance, and that our man in black really has a heart of gold and the interests of the country at heart. Right?'

'Well, yes, he did put that over,' admitted Tony.

'To give it force, he goes out leaving us alive,' continued Dawlish. 'There is a second string to his bow though. With us alive we'll report what he said. There's a chance that we'll report exactly what happened, and that the authorities will slacken off because of it.'

'No, hold it,' objected Tony. 'The police—'

'Not the police, they'll keep at it, of course. I'm thinking of my department. What you and I and Elvira have just heard is an attempt to bluff us off the case. He knows as well as I do where I come from.'

Elvira looked up.

'Aren't you just wonderful?' she said sarcastically. 'What a marvellous mind you must have!'

Dawlish put his head on one side.

'Elvira, that wasn't worthy of you. You can do much better than that. Among other things,' he added without a change of expression, 'you can add to our store of knowledge by telling us just why you went to Hennessy's house as a maid. Your uncle tried hard, but he didn't quite put it over. Why did you go?'

CHAPTER TWELVE

ELVIRA WILL NOT TALK

Elvira eyed him without speaking for some seconds, then deliberately turned and finished bathing Rennett's temple. Neither Dawlish nor Grayling moved. There was silence in the room, and with the silence there was tension.

The girl's face was set when she turned about.

'I've heard quite enough from you,' she said.

'But I haven't heard quite enough from you,' protested Dawlish.

'I won't be called a liar, and I won't have my uncle's story dismissed so casually,' she said. Her eyes glinted angrily. 'He is unconscious now, but if he were awake he—'

Dawlish raised his eyebrows.

'No doubt. No doubt. But you see, Elvira, he *is* unconscious, and I don't propose to wait much longer before hearing the truth. You've played a peculiar little game of your own and it's time for a showdown.'

She said: 'Get out of my way.'

Dawlish said evenly: 'Why did you go to Hennessy's?'

Elvira took a firm hold on the bowl of water.

'Move aside,' she said deliberately, 'or I'll throw this over you.'

'The child has a temper,' said Dawlish. He moved aside as she walked across the room and into the bathroom opposite.

Tony said uneasily:

'Pat, hadn't you better ease off? I mean, it was a pretty straight story.'

'With omissions,' answered Dawlish. 'We haven't heard all of it, and we're going to have a good try to find out more whether it hurts Elvira's feelings or not. I'm going to throw a scare into her,' he murmured as she returned from the bathroom.

She approached them steadily.

Dawlish let her pass, and then took her wrist. She tried to snatch it away, but his hold was firm.

'Let me go!'

'Later,' said Dawlish, gently. 'Why did you work for Hennessy?'

'You've already heard that!'

'Not the real reason.' Dawlish strengthened his grip.

'Let—me—go.'

'No,' said Dawlish. 'Elvira, I've been good to you so far. I don't know whether you understand what I am and what powers I have. You seem to have heard a little about me, and you and your uncle made a point of saying—'

She raised her free hand, and brought it sharply across his face.

Dawlish made no attempt to evade the blow. The marks of her fingers were on his cheek, as he caught and held her wrist.

He said sternly: 'Elvira, I have one job—to get results. I don't care how I get them. I can adopt any method I think fit, the only thing I have to answer for is the result. If you tell me the truth, all of it, not little oddments, you can stay here.

If you don't, you're coming with me. Make your choice. I am leaving in ten minutes.'

She said quickly: 'You can't make me come.'

Dawlish said:

'There aren't such things as concentration camps in England, Elvira, but there's a little place not far from here with accommodation for stubborn people. Quite a number of German spies are there, and sometimes someone gets in who isn't a spy, but who's acted suspiciously enough to be mistaken for one. It's quite unofficial, and the police would be shocked if they knew it existed, but—*my job is to get results*. Are you paying the place a visit, or are you going to be sensible?'

She drew a deep breath.

Tony, watching Dawlish's face, was almost convinced that he meant what he said. Dawlish's face was expressionless, his eyes narrowed and very hard. It was easy to imagine that he would let nothing stand in his way. He was frightening, then, more frightening than the man in black.

His hands gripped Elvira's tightly.

She said at last: 'You know why I went to Hennessy's.'

'I don't,' said Dawlish. 'Is that your last word?'

'Yes, damn you, yes!'

'You've had your chance,' said Dawlish. 'Hold her, Tony.'

Tony gripped her shoulders, but not tightly enough. She broke away. The first note of a scream began, but Tony put a hand across her mouth and the sound dropped to a faint gurgle.

Then she bit Tony's hand.

Dawlish took a small case from his pocket, opened it, and extracted a hypodermic syringe. He said sharply:

'Her forearm will do.'

'No,' gasped Elvira in a muffled voice, 'no, no! I'll tell you, I'll tell you!'

Dawlish kept the syringe in his hand as he said harshly:

'All right, what is the reason?'

Elvira glanced desperately towards her uncle, drew a sharp breath, and then wrenched herself away.

She slipped from Tony's grasp with such speed that he was left standing, and she flashed past Dawlish, who was taken completely by surprise. He grabbed at her but she escaped and reached the door. A second later her footsteps could be heard clattering down the stairs.

Dawlish was the first to rush after her.

The hall was gloomy, but he could see her running towards the front door.

He hurled himself in her wake as she went tearing along the short drive.

Reaching the gate, he was barely two yards behind her. Turning left too violently she fell.

Tony drew up alongside, the mad pursuit over.

'What's happened?'

'She slipped.'

'Pat, I hope you know what you're doing.'

Dawlish did not answer, but bent down and lifted the girl. She was not unconscious, but kept still enough as he carried her back to the house.

In the hall, Tony closed the door and switched on the light. Dawlish put Elvira on a chair, and stared down at her.

'Now we know that you were lying.'

Elvira kept silent.

Dawlish went on: 'You're asking for serious trouble, Elvira. I haven't the slightest doubt that you think you're protecting your uncle, but you're wrong.'

'I've—I've nothing to say.'

Dawlish shrugged.

'All right, you've asked for it.'

'What the devil are you going to do?' demanded Tony. 'Look here, Pat, you can't go too far!'

Dawlish turned on him sharply.

'I'm going to take Elvira away,' he said, 'and unless she talks, she'll stay away. Her uncle won't be able to contact her, and one or the other of them will crack. Don't argue, old man, it is her own choice, not mine.'

He had the syringe in his hand again when there was a call from upstairs. Dawlish hesitated, and Elvira stood up unsteadily. She said:

'You'd better—ask him.'

Tony helped her upstairs in Dawlish's wake, but on the threshold of the bedroom Dawlish turned and raised a hand. Alone he went into the bedroom and closed the door.

Rennett was sitting up on the pillows, pale and ill.

'Where's Vi?' he snapped.

'She's under arrest,' said Dawlish shortly.

'Under *what!*'

'You heard me.'

'Look here, Dawlish.' Rennett pressed a hand against his forehead. 'What the devil are you talking about? Elvira's done nothing.'

'Then you have, and she's paying for it.'

Rennett stared at him, breathing heavily. The contusions on his temple looked red and angry, but the rest of his face was unnaturally pale.

'Let the girl alone,' he growled.

'I don't know what will happen to her,' said Dawlish. 'I do know that you won't see her again until you've told me why she went to work for Hennessy. You put up a good show but not good enough. You lied and she backed you up. But the game's over, Rennett. We're not playing now.'

Rennett said in a low voice:

'If you hurt that girl I'll kill you, Dawlish.'

'Histrionics apart, why did you send her to work for Hennessy?' demanded Dawlish. Under his harsh persistence was a real fear that Rennett would remain silent. It was possible that his part in the affair was irrelevant to the main issue. But he must know. Nor was he any keener than Grayling on bullying Elvira.

Rennett said explosively:

'Damn you, Dawlish, I'll get even with you one day. Where is she?'

'At the moment, outside.'

'Is she hurt?'

'She fell and banged her head. When I tried to make her tell me why she went to The Lees, she ran away. That wasn't wise, for it confirmed my belief that you'd been lying. What is the truth, Rennett?'

'Bring her in here, and I'll tell you,' growled Rennett.

Dawlish called out to the others, and they came in. Rennett stared tight-lipped towards Elvira, but made no mention of the bruise on her forehead or her pallor. Harshly he said:

'Good girl, I knew I could trust you. But we've got to tell them, we can't make more trouble.'

He turned to Dawlish.

'Remember what I told you about Hennessy abroad?' he demanded abruptly. 'That was true. Everything was true, except that I had a damned sight stronger reason for wanting Elvira at The Lees than I told you. Hennessy and I have hated each other all our lives. I've never trusted the man, and I don't now. In Singapore there was a big robbery, from the native jewel-market. I was convinced that Hennessy was mixed up in it, and I knew he dealt in stones. I wanted Elvira there to find where he kept his stuff, so that I could have a look at it. If you want to know whether that's the truth or not, you'll find some Singapore papers, mentioning the robbery, in that dressing-table.

Dawlish rubbed the side of his nose thoughtfully, and after a pause spoke mildly enough.

'Is that all?'

'Isn't it enough?'

'I don't see why you were so anxious that I shouldn't know about it.

'You don't?' Rennett barked. 'Have you got any idea that Singapore is in Jap hands now? Fifty thousand pounds worth of gems came out of Singapore, and their owners are either dead or prisoners. I'm told the market was blown sky-high in one of the bombing attacks.' Bennett swallowed, and then went on defiantly: 'I'm not a rich man, Dawlish. If I'd laid my hands on those stolen gems I would have known how to use them.'

Elvira said swiftly.

'That isn't the whole truth, Uncle.'

'You be quiet,' growled Rennett. 'Don't try to whitewash me. Dawlish is a born sceptic with an inborn suspicion of the stuff.'

Dawlish was thinking of the story, and the probability that it was true. He felt a curious sense of deflation. It was possible that the gems, if they existed, provided motive enough for what had happened. He thought of the man in black and his statement that it was a matter of private vengeance and saw the possibility that his earlier ideas were wrong, and that this was, in fact, merely a matter for the police.

Then he heard Elvira say:

'We lost practically everything in Singapore and Malaya. Uncle had all his savings in Malayan rubber stocks. He knows that the man who lost most of the jewels is dead. He only meant to keep a few of them, just enough to pay his expenses until this house is sold and I've found something to do, and he can get to sea again.' She looked into Dawlish's face, and then exclaimed: 'It's true! We had to work on our own, if we'd told the police what we planned they would never have believed us!'

'Nor does he,' growled Rennett. 'Not that he can do anything about it,' the sailor added. 'The only thing he *can* do is to stop you going back to Hennessy.'

Dawlish said:

'That's over, anyhow. Our visitor told Hennessy who Elvira is.'

Rennett stared at him, speechless.

'Well?' said Elvira, into the following pause. 'What are you going to do?'

'Do?' asked Dawlish absently. 'There's nothing for me to do, except to admonish you, my sweet, for excessive loyalty. Have either of you ever heard any rumour about Hennessy being involved in espionage?'

'If I had,' said Rennett promptly, 'the police would certainly have been told.'

Dawlish shrugged.

'Ah, well, it's possible that you'll have other visitors. I think someone might wish to kill you.' He smiled bleakly. 'Watch your step, Rennett. Elvira, be careful.'

He moved to the door, Tony following him.

Downstairs, Tony said:

'Are you really going to leave it just like that, Pat?'

'Of course not,' said Dawlish quietly. 'We may have all the truth, I think perhaps we have, but I also think that they're in danger. So one of us has to go hungry for a bit longer, and this time I think I'll do the hanging about. Go back to the hotel, old man. Telephone the flat as soon as you get there, and ask Ted to come down here at once. If by any chance Tim Jeremy has turned up, tell him to come too. Is that clear?'

'What are you going to do?'

'Wait and watch,' said Dawlish, 'until you've had some food. Don't make it too long.'

It was nearly an hour and a half before Tony returned.

During the whole of that time Dawlish had been patrolling the house, his footsteps softened by the grass.

No one had left, nor had anyone entered.

Tony did not drive the Lagonda right up to the door, but stopped it some distance away. Dawlish heard the familiar note of the engine, and walked swiftly along the verge, meeting Tony in the gateway.

'Anything?' asked Tony swiftly.

'Nothing. Did you get the message through?'

'Yes. Ted and Tim are coming down right away.'

'Good man. How are the others?'

Tony chuckled. 'Bored, I gathered.'

'That won't do 'em any harm,' said Dawlish. 'I haven't seen any movement here, and I've a feeling there won't be any from the inside, although our gent in black may return. The moon is just coming up,' he added, 'and you'll find it easy to watch.'

'I'll be all right,' said Tony confidently. 'A jolly good meal inside me, I feel a new man.'

Dawlish chuckled.

But he was not smiling when he walked softly along the pavement, seeing the dark shape of the Lagonda thirty feet along the road. Tony on his own might be enough to withstand any attack on Rennett or Elvira; but on the other hand if there was an attack in strength, one man could do little. He wondered whether he would be wise to get in touch with the local police and ask them to stand guard also.

Irritably, he let in the clutch.

He could not make up his mind whether further precautions

at 18a, The Grove, were necessary or not, until he reached the main road and the headlamps of his car showed the outlines of a telephone kiosk. He pulled up, went in, and called the police station. In a few seconds he learned that it was known that he was in Bournemouth, and he was offered exactly the same co-operation as by the Dorset Police.

'Yes, of course,' said the Inspector to whom he spoke. 'We'll station four men in The Grove at once.'

Dawlish ran a hand over his hair as he left the kiosk, and was very thoughtful as he stepped into the Lagonda. The ease with which that had gone through was bewildering. Earlier the co-operation of the Dorset Police had been less surprising, for he had been concerned with crime of which they knew. Now it seemed clear that a word had been spoken from some high authority, and the police were sufficiently impressed to say 'That's perfectly all right, sir.'

'It's damned odd,' Dawlish confided to the controls.

At the hotel, a meal had been kept on a hot-plate for him. Attended by an aged waiter, he ate alone, then went to his room and laid full length on the bed. Still puzzled by the affability of the police, he concentrated as much on that as on anything which had happened.

It was eleven o'clock. Ted and Tim Jeremy could not be expected until one at the earliest, and they might be an hour later. He arranged with the night porter to be called at two o'clock, or when the others arrived, whichever was the sooner, then took off his outer clothes and climbed into bed.

He was asleep within a few minutes, and slept heavily.

He was awakened by a tap on the door, and then a deep voice, booming:

'Come on, you blighter, that's enough shut-eye for one night.'

Into the room stepped Timothy Jeremy, a large, spare-boned man with an engaging grin.

'Well, well!' he said. 'Captain Dawlish in *décolleté*! Hallo, Pat!'

Behind the speaker loomed Ted Beresford.

Hurriedly Dawlish dressed and took them down to the resident's lounge.

It took him twenty minutes to give them a résumé of what had happened. They said little, although once or twice Tim grunted satisfaction or the reverse. When it was finished Ted said slowly:

'What do you make of it, Pat?'

'I'm not too happy,' admitted Dawlish. 'Outside of anything that's happened, there's a queer state of affairs. Everyone in authority defers to me, and I don't like it. It's much too easy.' He shrugged. 'Just ask yourselves whether Whitehead would have been able to get co-operation like this solely on the strength of what I've told him? He didn't say that he knew anything else, but he worked damned fast and thoroughly. I don't like being kept in the dark,' he added, 'and there's something here they haven't told me.'

'It could be,' admitted Ted. 'What are you going to do?'

'I'm going to see Whitehead,' said Dawlish, 'and find out just what's behind it. Or try to,' he added with a grin. 'Now, you two—'

He talked for five minutes, telling them what to do at The Grove, and of the arrangement he had made with the police. Just before three o'clock they set off with detailed instructions on how to reach Rennett's house.

Dawlish ran the Lagonda out, and relocked the garage.

He knew the road well enough to make good speed once he was beyond Christchurch. Sometimes an army lorry rumbled towards him, and several times commercial vehicles dropped behind him.

By now the moon was at its height, bathing the countryside in its soft glow, accentuating the tall forms of trees which rose on either side. He drove through a patch of wooded country, then slowed down, approaching a village. The headlights of his car shone on the windows of a house as he turned a corner; it was the last house of the village, and he opened out again.

He had not gone fifty yards before a tyre burst. The wheels skidded and the steering wheel was jerked from his hand. He grabbed it and straightened out, but while he was doing so he saw figures running towards him from the hedges.

CHAPTER THIRTEEN

ROADSIDE ATTACK

Things happened so swiftly that Dawlish had little time to think, only to realize that he was in a dangerous spot.

Snatching up his revolver he fired blindly through the window in the direction of the moving figures.

There was a shout, and a man fell.

At least six others were advancing. As Dawlish opened his door they rushed the car. Something pricked into Dawlish's arm.

He felt his senses reeling, knew that he was losing consciousness, and for a few brief seconds tried to fight against it.

The he slumped forward over the steering wheel.

The man in black sat in an easy chair in a house on the outskirts of Lyndhurst. Opposite him was the little man who had accompanied him to The Grove. He was grinning widely.

'We got him, it was easy.'

'As easy as all that?' asked the man in black.

'Sure, sure,' said the little man. 'He wasn't expecting it. Topsy got a bullet in the thigh, but there wasn't any more damage, and no one followed us. It's okay.'

'Take him upstairs,' ordered the man in black, 'and don't let him see you.'

'I know what I'm about,' said the little man. 'Trust me, Boss, I'll fix it.' He winked, and then went out jauntily. The man in black, whose face was still curiously white and motionless, leaned forward and pressed a bell.

After a short interval the door opened again.

Into the room stepped another man, as small, but bald-headed and much older than the first.

'Have you got him, Jamie?'

'We've got him,' said the man in black sombrely.

'I'm looking forward to a talk with Dawlish,' said the other, rubbing his hands together. 'If Bateson hadn't—'

'We needn't go into that,' said the man called 'Jamie'. 'You know what to do?'

'Of course I do.'

'It may be better if I were to go through the instructions again,' 'Jamie' said slowly. Although the uncanny immobility of his features remained, he spoke in a natural, rather husky voice. 'Dawlish will not, of course, know that I am interested in him. You will tell him the story which we have prepared.'

He talked for another five minutes, and then the bald-headed man nodded, stood up, and went out.

Some twenty minutes later he entered a room on the top floor of the house. On a bed in one corner lay Dawlish. He was awake, but his hands were bound and there was adhesive tape over his lips.

The little man pulled at the adhesive tape.

He worked gently; that surprised Dawlish, who knew how painful the operation could be. The tape pulled at his skin, but the pain was negligible.

The little man took an automatic from his pocket, and a

hypodermic syringe. These he placed on a small table, near his hand.

'Now, Captain Dawlish,' began the little man portentously. 'I have some things to say to you.'

Dawlish said mildly: 'And I to you, Polly.'

The little man's expression altered; it had been bland, but now it grew tense and angry. He leaned forward with a hand outstretched, and Dawlish expected a blow. It did not come; the man sat back, and then said harshly:

'You don't know what you're talking about.'

'You'd be surprised what I know,' said Dawlish quietly. 'You and yours make so many mistakes.'

'Shut your mouth!' snapped the other.

'Come, we all learn by our mistakes,' said Dawlish.

The man moved his hand again, and this time the blow fell, and Dawlish's head jerked back.

'Another mistake, Polly, as you may live to learn.'

The man stood up abruptly. It was easy to see that he was trying to repress an outbreak of fury. He succeeded, although his voice was thick as he went on:

'You'll be funny once too often. What did you find out from Rennett?'

'Rennett?'

The man snapped: 'Did he tell you where they are?'

'Where what are?'

There was a pause, while the man stepped to the table and picked up the hypodermic syringe.

'Now listen to me, Dawlish, and get this straight. I can do what I like with you. I can kill you and get rid of your body, and I won't be caught. Even if I *was* caught, it wouldn't help you.'

Dawlish said absently: '*Were* caught.'

'What?'

'Just a matter of grammar,' said Dawlish. 'You should have said: "if I were caught". It's not important, I gather your meaning, but it just shows you how easy these mistakes are.'

The man clenched his fists.

'*You're* making a mistake,' he said softly. 'You're making a big one, Dawlish. I can kill you and no one will be any the wiser for a long time. You've got just one chance of getting away alive.'

'By George!' exclaimed Dawlish. 'Pass it on, I can use it!'

There was another silence, while Dawlish wondered whether he was trying the other too far. His facetiousness was deliberately enraging, and might prove dangerous; but it was giving him time to assess the situation, and his head was clearing.

He did not feel anything like as casual as he sounded; there was an unpleasant heaviness in his chest, and he did not doubt that the other would have few scruples about killing. If there were a problem, it was why he had been allowed to live for so long.

'The next time you interrupt I'll bash your face in,' said 'Polly' viciously. 'Don't make any mistake about that.' He picked up the automatic by the barrel, and swished it through the air, so that it passed within an inch of Dawlish's nose.

'Now listen to me, Dawlish. You've got just one chance of coming out of this alive. I know what Rennett's done, but I don't know where he's put the stuff. Did you get it out of him?'

Dawlish said: 'What stuff?'

'The jewels.'

'This is a new one on me,' said Dawlish quietly.

'That's a lie,' snapped 'Polly'. 'You needn't think we don't know what you're after, Dawlish. You're after the jewels. Rennett's got them, or he knows where they are.' The man took a step forward, and pointed the butt of the gun towards Dawlish. 'There's a hundred thousand pounds-worth of jewels, and I'm going to get them!'

Dawlish looked at the gun, thinking:

'A hundred thousand pounds this time. Rennett said fifty thousand. I wonder what idea there is behind this?'

'I'm going to get them,' went on 'Polly'. 'Don't make any mistake about that. I'm not the only one looking for them, and I'm not a killer, but if it comes to it I'll kill to get my hands on those jewels. What did Rennett tell you?'

'Nothing about jewels,' lied Dawlish.

He repeated the story which Rennett had told him, with some reservations, and only up to the point where the man in black had interrupted. As the story progressed, the man nodded frequently, and did not appear dissatisfied.

Dawlish finished:

'That's all I know, Polly, take it or leave it.'

'That's what you say,' said 'Polly' with a sudden glitter in his eyes. 'Who are you working for?'

Dawlish said: 'Don't you know?'

'If it's who I think it is, you're through,' said Polly viciously. 'The man who killed Beth Arthurson, I know. You go around in a uniform and pretend you're a swell, but you're just a double-crossing two-timing crook, I know your kind. I wish I had Kohn where I've got you,' he added harshly.

Dawlish said quietly: 'Who's Kohn?' but remembered Trivett's talk of the dangerous brother of the dead Kohn named by Bateson.

'Don't come your clever stuff with me,' sneered 'Polly'. 'Kohn's your boss. Next time you see him tell him that he can wipe the paint off his face, I know who he is.'

'I haven't the faintest idea who you're talking about,' said Dawlish, but his heart was beating fast.

Polly peered closer to Dawlish's face, and then exclaimed: 'I believe that's the truth, I believe you're a dick. God!'

There followed a tense silence.

'God!' gasped 'Polly' again, 'I can see it now. I—' He stopped abruptly, then backed away. 'So that's it, you thought you'd double-cross me that way. Listen, Dawlish, this hypo hasn't got a knock-out drop this time, it will kill you.' He grabbed the syringe, staring furiously down at Dawlish. 'Are you working with Kohn or aren't you? Tell me the truth, are you working with Kohn?'

Dawlish said: 'I'm working with no one.'

'You—' gasped 'Polly'. 'You devil, you're a dick, that's what you are!'

Then he plunged the needle of the syringe into Dawlish's arm.

On the fringes of the New Forest three men were busily clearing the scrub. They worked without speaking, their spades striking against stones from time to time, making a clear, ringing tone.

One of the men stopped and brushed his hand over his forehead, his glance rested on a shed some fifty yards away.

'It's time fer brekker, Joe.'

'In a minute,' said one of the others.

'I'm that thirsty,' said the first speaker, 'I'm not waiting for un.' He pushed his spade into the earth, wiped his forehead again, and made for the hut. Rummaging in a basket, he stood at the doorway with a bottle in his hand.

He pulled out the cork with a grunt of satisfaction.

'Ar,' he said aloud. 'That's good. Perishing hot it'll be today, I reckon. I—'

He stopped abruptly, his eyes fixed on a small clearing in the nearby trees. The others, approaching him, saw the expression on his face, and turned to look in the same direction.

Stretched on the ground was the body of a man.

'You see what *I* see?' exclaimed the first speaker.

'Aye, I see un,' said Joe. 'Come on, don't stand gawking, man.' He led the way towards the clearing, and when they were a few yards away from the outstretched man he added: 'Looks a big feller.'

'Aye.'

There were no signs of violence, but the man, in officer's uniform, was unconscious. Joe felt his wrist with a soil-stained hand.

'It's not beating so good.'

'Better get the police.'

'And a doctor,' said Joe. 'Hurry after un, this fellow needs looking after.' He scratched his head. 'Wonder how he got there,' he said. 'Funny place to get to, if you ask me.'

The third man was already on a bicycle pedalling over the uneven ground towards Lyndhurst, three miles along the road. The sun rose higher and the mists cleared, while by the hut where the men had carried him, Dawlish lay unconscious.

CHAPTER FOURTEEN

NEWS FROM WHITEHEAD

Ted Beresford eased his large body out of his car, stood for a moment in front of the Jermyn Street house, then stepped into the hall. He was half-way up the stairs when the door opened, and Felicity appeared.

'How is he?'

'So-so,' said Beresford.

'No better than that?'

'He's still unconscious,' said Beresford. He laid a hand on Felicity's arm, and led her back into the flat. 'If I know Pat he'll pull through all right. He's in a nursing home not far from where they found him this morning.'

Felicity said determinedly: 'I'm going down there.'

'I don't think you should, Fel,' said Beresford slowly. 'They've promised to have him brought to London if he can be moved, and I don't think there's any sense in going down. I mean—'

Felicity said: 'Ted, don't try to talk me out of it, and tell me the truth. Is he any worse?'

'No.' Beresford was emphatic. 'He hasn't changed since they found him. I've arranged with the matron of the home to ring through here if there's any change, or'—he paused—'any need to send for you. They don't think he's in acute danger. As far as I can see they can't make out what the trouble is. Anyhow, they've sent for Betteridge, and he's on his way there now. Tim's waiting for word from him before telephoning. If you must go down,' Beresford added, 'make it after Betteridge's report.'

Felicity looked at the large man squarely. 'Ted, is he badly hurt? Has he been knocked about? Is that the trouble?'

'Good Lord, no!' exclaimed Beresford. 'There's hardly a scratch on him. Listen to me, Fel. There's only one reason why I don't want you to go down there, and it's simple enough. You might meet trouble on the way. In the same circumstances Pat would say "stay put", and you know it. In any case,' added Beresford with greater confidence than he felt, 'he'll probably be in London within twenty-four hours.'

Very reluctantly, Felicity agreed to wait.

At half past three Robbie Graham came in and slumped down disconsolately.

'All these things happen in the course of a couple of days, and then we come to a dead stop. I can't even think why!'

Ted grinned.

'Pat's been the thinking machine of this outfit too long to change it, Robbie, and he'll be around soon. I've told you pretty well everything that Tony told me. What do you make of it?'

'That's the trouble, I can make no sense of anything,' said Robbie.

Felicity said quietly: 'As far as I can make out, everything turns on this story about jewels from Singapore.'

'Jewels!' snorted Robbie. 'How does that tie-up with the fact that they knew what boat I was on?'

'How does it tie-up with you at all?' asked Felicity.

'He's probably the master-crook,' grinned Beresford. 'We'd better turn out his pockets and see if they're full of sparklers.'

'You're a mutton-headed lout,' declared Robbie laconically, 'how Fel stands you I don't know. Look here, why don't you go to see Whitewash, or whatever his name is? You're in his office, aren't you? He'll tell you something, surely?'

Superintendent Trivett was expressing a similar question to Sir Archibald Morely, the Assistant Commissioner of Police at Scotland Yard.

Sitting in Morely's office and looking into the thin face of the A.C., a man who looked younger than his forty-odd years, Trivett complained with some bitterness. From the start they had been compelled to work under instructions from Whitehead's department. It was one thing to give a *carte blanche* to Dawlish: that had been done often enough, and he had never failed them yet, but Whitehead had had little to do with the police until this affair, and they considered they had been kept unnecessarily in the dark.

'It isn't only us,' said Trivett. 'The Dorset and Hampshire people are in the same boat. So are the Surrey men. They've had these orders to watch the people on the list, but apart from what Dawlish told me, and that's precious little, we don't know a thing.'

'Well, if it's any consolation to you, I don't like it any more than you do,' said Morely.

'It's so damned unfair!' exclaimed Trivett. 'We might get a lot of information from these people if we could, question them, but all we have to do is to watch and wait.'

Morely smiled faintly.

'You're not going to tell me that you don't know why that is, Trivett.'

Trivett shrugged his shoulders irritably.

'That's obvious enough,' he admitted. 'Colonel Whitehead doesn't want these people to know that they're being watched.

He expects further attacks. If the others have been attacked, then the two people in London and the two in Surrey might be. But it's an invidious position for us, sir.'

Quietly Morely lifted the telephone and ordered some tea.

'You know, Trivett, you're really annoyed because they haven't taken us into their confidence. I don't think they told Dawlish much, either; he hasn't acted as if he knows a great deal. There's more in this than meets the eye. As far as our part goes, if we prevent any attack on the people we're watching, and hold anyone who tries such an attack, then we can't grumble and nor can they.' He paused as the telephone rang, and lifted the receiver. 'Hallo? . . . Who? . . . Why yes.' There was a hint of excitement in his voice. 'Bring him along immediately.' He glanced at Trivett. 'Colonel Whitehead's coming in now, we might learn more.' He lifted the receiver again, and said: 'Ask the canteen to make that tea for three, will you? Thanks.'

Trivett raised one eyebrow above the other.

'The first thing he'll do is to ask me if I'll go out,' he said sourly.

He was wrong. Colonel Whitehead entered with a bland smile turned equally on Morely and on Trivett.

'Well, now, it's time I told you people what I can.'

'We'd just reached the same conclusion,' said Morely drily. 'But first, how is Dawlish?'

'I'm expecting word of him any time,' said Whitehead. 'It was a bad business, but I have great faith in his powers of recovery. So have his friends, I gather. If he had a complaint, it was that I hadn't told him why I acted as I did, and you people probably feel the same.' Whitehead smiled. 'That isn't a difficult question to answer. I didn't know.'

Morely stared at him, and Trivett's handsome face expressed acute surprise.

'Well, there it is,' Whitehead went on. 'You know how Dawlish got on to this business, don't you? Picked it out of the air, so to speak. Now believe it or not, Graham came back to England for no reason at all, except that several officers were due for a refresher course and he was chosen as one of them. So whatever the mystery is, Graham's not in it, *if* it's espionage.'

'There's talk of jewels,' Trivett said cautiously.

'So I've heard,' nodded Whitehead. 'And as far as they are concerned, we should, of course keep an open mind. And we have to admit one cogent fact. Graham was known to be returning. Someone who should not have given that information did so. Whatever the circumstances, the fact remains that there was a serious leakage of official information.'

'Unless it's on this side, it's hardly our field,' Morely said.

'I know that, Morely, I know it only too well,' said Whitehead. 'However, it does link up with the murders in Dorset, which *are* in your field. Dawlish is the liaison officer between us, and I hope he isn't laid up for too long.'

He broke off, as a constable came in with a tray of tea and biscuits.

'What I was going to say,' continued Whitehead, accepting a cup of rich brown brew, 'is that I wanted Dawlish to do what he thought best, and I have your assurance that I couldn't choose a better man. I wanted the other people watched by you, and I wanted to find whether any of the people on the list Dawlish obtained have ever been suspected of espionage by my men. There have been vague suspicions of one of them—Hennessy. He was in Singapore, as the report from Dawlish's friend tells us, and at that time there was a jewel robbery which created a considerable sensation. But what Dawlish was not told, apparently, is that there was something else stolen.'

Trivett and Morely stared into their cups woodenly.

'There were papers stolen,' Whitehead continued. 'For a long time our intelligence people in Malaya and Singapore had been preparing a list of suspected fifth columnists. It was proposed to arrest the men the moment there was any immediate threat of a Japanese attack. The list was deliberately kept piecemeal, so that no single copy could be taken. Now on the very day that all these lists had been turned over to the Senior Officer for the first time, they were stolen. There were three lots, kept in three places. All of them went, all three of them!'

Whitehead stopped.

There was a complete silence in the office, the tea cooling unheeded.

It was Morely who broke the silence.

'What happened then?'

Whitehead shrugged.

'The obvious thing. The named people were warned by someone, and disappeared. A few detentions were made, but very few. Some of the men who had been compiling the record were murdered, and twelve months work was lost in a few hours. When eventually the attack came the place was littered with spies and fifth columnists, it was one of the biggest factors in the loss of the Settlements.' Whitehead raised his cup to his lips and put it down quickly. 'Well, that's the connection between espionage and the jewels we've heard about. Big enough, you'll admit. But it isn't all,' he added quietly. 'It isn't all by a long way. There was a similar trouble in Burma, and still is, and of course the problem assumes gigantic proportions in India.'

'India!' echoed Trivett.

'That's right, Superintendent,' said Whitehead heavily. 'The organisation which smashed our espionage work in the Settlements went a long way towards smashing it in Burma.

Obviously it's the work of people who are now preparing and operating the fifth column in Burma and India.'

'Ye-es,' said Morely slowly.

'And now for some reason or other there is trouble in England, possibly connected with it. I say possibly because we can't be sure, yet, although we can reach logical conclusions. Would you say that espionage is a more reasonable explanation of the ruthless behaviour of the men we are fighting than a few paltry jewels?' He paused, and then went on heavily: 'Of course you would. I don't pretend to see the connection yet, but I do believe that someone in this country, probably someone on Bateson's list, can give information which would enable us to strike at the organisation in India. I can't go any further than that.'

'I see,' said Morely. He paused, and then added: 'What do you propose to do?'

CHAPTER FIFTEEN

ARREST THE LOT?

The question of what he was going to do did not rest solely with Colonel Whitehead. He told Morely and Trivett that he was to attend a conference shortly, and was considering the idea of arresting or detaining all the people on Bateson's list. There was the alternative suggestion of waiting for further attacks on them in hopes of trapping the assailants. He believed that was the system on which Dawlish would work.

'It probably is,' admitted Trivett. 'But there's one thing about Dawlish which you mustn't forget, sir.'

'What's that?' demanded Whitehead sharply.

'He takes big chances,' said Trivett. He smiled a little and went on: 'Don't misunderstand me, I have a great faith in Dawlish, and if the risks paid off it would be O.K. On the other hand, if he took risks in this instance, and lost, the consequences might be irreparable.'

Whitehead nodded. 'True. What do you think, Morely?'

'I wish Dawlish were here,' said Morely worriedly. 'He might have learned a great deal before being knocked out. If I had to make a decision at the moment, it would be: wait for twenty-four hours to see whether Dawlish can tell us anything.'

'That's my view, too,' admitted Whitehead. 'I think I'll recommend that course.'

He left soon afterwards, and went to his office. From there he was summoned to the conference. All were aware of the grave issues at stake as argument and discussion continued. At last Whitehead said quietly:

'Gentlemen, I think you've forgotten one thing. Had Dawlish not been impressed by Graham's story, and acted as he did, we should have no idea at all of what was happening. I think we can say that Dawlish has forced these people into the open, and has built something out of nothing.'

'What has that to do with our decision?' asked the representative from the India Office testily.

'A great deal, I think,' said Whitehead. 'If we'd known nothing, we could have done nothing. We would have been completely in the dark. Now, because we know a little, we are tempted to act precipitously. We are in a much better position than we were forty-eight hours ago, and a delay of twenty-four hours won't alter that. I think we should wait that time for Dawlish.'

'You seem to have great faith in this man Dawlish,' said the representative from I.O., with some sarcasm.

The Rt. Hon. Jonathan Scott, Minister for War, looked sharply across the table.

'Dawlish has done astonishing things before. I think he will again. I'm for giving him the chance.'

Whitehead waited in some concern for a vote to be taken. Only the Indian Office representative was for immediate arrests; the others gave Dawlish twenty-four hours in which to recover enough to offer suggestions.

With a sigh of profound relief Whitehead went back to his

office. There was a chit of paper tucked into the corner of his blotting pad. It read:

Telephoned at 4.45 p.m. Captain Dawlish is conscious, and being moved to London.

Robbie Graham was amazed.

Since word had come from Tim Jeremy that Dawlish was conscious and already on his way to Town the whole atmosphere of the flat had changed. The very voices of the occupants had grown lighter, gayer.

'Robbie,' Beresford told him, looking down on the youngster's chubby face, 'Six times—*six times*—Pat has been involved in shows similar to this. He's got through. He'll get through now. God knows what's behind it, but I think it's pretty big. If Pat had been out of action for a few weeks, it might have got out of hand. He won't be. Betteridge says that he should be all right in forty-eight hours. Knowing Pat, the forty-eight will be twenty-four, and when he gets over this, things will begin to happen.'

Robbie glanced at Felicity, and saw that she was smiling.

'Good Lord!' he said helplessly. 'You really believe it.'

He did not say it in so many words, but the evidence of their belief in Dawlish cheered him mightily. A little later, when Tim Jeremy entered, booming about the flat demanding first beer and then food, he saw that he, too, was as confident as the others.

Meanwhile Dawlish lay in a nursing home in central London, feeling terrible. He had the worst headache he could remember, and every limb throbbed, stung, hurt, and refused to move at his direction. But his mind worked freely enough.

He knew what had happened.

Betteridge had diagnosed a drug not unlike evipan, and had assured him that in all probability he would be back to normal in a few days. Dawlish had said little, but while he lay in the nursing home he was going through everything he had heard and said and done.

By eleven o'clock that night he was feeling better.

Felicity had been to see him, and stayed for half an hour. Tony and Ted had looked in, and Whitehead was due at eleven-fifteen. Until then, Dawlish had said nothing of what had happened to him.

He had arranged for Tim and Ted to be in the room, and when they arrived, all three together, he grinned crookedly at the Colonel and said:

'I'm all ears.'

Whitehead scowled at him.

'And so am I, Dawlish. I'm waiting to hear what you have to say first.'

Dawlish shook his head.

'Of course, sir, if you insist. *But—*'

Whitehead chuckled.

'I told you that you could do what you like, and I won't back out of that. All right, Dawlish—'

He told them what he had told Trivett and Morely. Watching Dawlish's face, he was surprised to see that it was without expression.

'Well, Dawlish, how much of that surprises you?'

'Surprises?' repeated Dawlish. 'Why, none of it, it's exactly what I was looking for.'

'Oh,' said Whitehead blankly.

Dawlish raised himself on his pillows.

'It's obvious that the jewels covered something else. If a man went to rob Mrs. Arthurson, knowing she had those jewels, he might have killed her in a fit of violence. But there was no robbery, there were no signs at all that the place had been searched. She was killed simply because she knew something. They tried to get Hennessy, or pretended to. And Pollittzer—I'm going to be surprised if he wasn't murdered.'

'He was,' said Whitehead in a small voice. 'An over-dose of adrenalin by hypodermic injection given presumably while mixing with a crowd.'

'Well, that's two murders,' said Dawlish crisply, surprised that he was feeling so much better. 'Two murders to prevent people talking. No robbery, unless anything's been reported?' He looked at Whitehead.

'I've had no such report,' admitted the Colonel.

'Good. A series of threats, in the form of a terrorist campaign,' went on Dawlish. 'Some barefaced effrontery, for the shabby little cove and the others have taken enormous chances. Add them all up together, and you certainly don't get a jewel robbery motive. Of course, Polly tried to convince me that was what he was after.' He closed his eyes. 'At my last inter-view with—'

He stopped, realising that he had not yet talked of the attack on the road and the ensuing conversation. He related the story briefly, and when he had finished went on:

'The little man pretended that the thought of me being a policeman was a surprise. What's more,' added Dawlish with a twisted smile, 'although he pumped the stuff into me, he let me live. The man in black did, too. Two men with but a single motive! They wanted to make me think the jewels were the major objective. What does that suggest?'

Whitehead eyed the big man curiously.

'I'm not going to try to guess. Do you seriously suggest that you can read anything into it?'

'Anything!' exclaimed Dawlish. 'Nearer everything, I think. Polly supported the man in black's jewel thesis, and then, by an astonishing display of melodrama, tried to convince me that he and the man in black were not working together.'

'What!' exclaimed Beresford.

'As you told the story, the man you call Polly was in no way connected with the man he called Kohn,' said Whitehead.

'I've told the story as it was given to me, but I can draw my own conclusions. Polly wanted me to think he was working independently of Kohn, of course. Polly wanted to convince me that two parties are working to get these precious jewels. Or three, for he implicated Rennett and Elvira. But the insistence on the jewel theme suggests that he and Kohn are working together. Or,' he demanded, eyeing Whitehead, 'am I being illogical?'

'No,' admitted Whitehead slowly.

'Good,' said Dawlish. 'The jewel theme is off, the fifth column organisation is on. Where do we get from that? Someone in this country knows a great deal about it, and must be stopped. A series of warnings is sent around. But,' he added gently, 'why in the name of St. Peter should people who kill like this satisfy themselves with giving warnings? It doesn't make sense.'

'Are you?' asked Tim Jeremy faintly.

'Work it out for yourself,' invited Dawlish. 'These people on Bateson's list *might* know something about the organisation. Kohn—we don't know for sure that our man is named Kohn, but we can't go on calling him the man in black, and it will do for the time being—Kohn, then, wanted to warn them not to talk. He did. Apparently he succeeded. Then Bateson slipped up, and we got the list. Kohn obviously saw the chance that Bateson would crack, and decided to act immediately. Until then, these half-dozen or so innocents weren't dangerous, but directly anyone began to interrogate them they would become so. He decided to get ahead of me, and kill them off. He wasn't quite fast enough, and was forced into the open. Everything considered,' added Dawlish, 'we're making progress. Of course we come back to the original problem—what do these people know?'

'Can you answer that one?' demanded Ted.

'Not yet. The only thing clear so far, is that four of them know one another, I think we ought to check that up further, sir. I suggest that the police find out from the others on the list whether they know Hennessy, Mrs. Arthurson, Rennett, and Pollittzer. Can you arrange that?'

'I will do,' promised Whitehead. He pushed his chair back. 'I think that's enough from you for tonight. Oh, I'd like you to know that there was a strong vote of confidence in you passed earlier today. I'm not at liberty to say what the meeting was, but it took place in a little street off Whitehall.' He smiled blandly and stood up. 'Do you think you can justify it, Dawlish?'

'I can try,' Dawlish said simply. 'One thing before you go, sir. Are all the people concerned being closely watched?'

'Very closely,' Whitehead assured him.

When Whitehead had gone, Tim and Ted eyed Dawlish expectantly. Neither of them spoke. Then Dawlish said mildly:

'Which of you is the more anxious to have his head blown off?'

'That's more like it,' said Ted. 'What do you want us to do?'

Dawlish said promptly:

'Go to the flat first. Ask Tony and Robbie to stay there, with Felicity, until I get over. Then you, Ted, go down to Dorset and join the police watching Hennessy's place. Tim, you go to Rennett's house at Westbourne. Get there as soon as you can, and just hang about until you hear from me, unless anything looks like happening. Use your own judgment if it does, and yell for the police if needs be.' He smiled when he finished, and settled back in the bed. 'Now I'm going to sleep,' he said. 'I haven't felt so tired for months.'

* * *

Dawn was breaking over the Lees when Beresford drew his car up fifty yards from the house. He had found it easy enough to reach Wimborne, but difficult to find The Lees. After wasting half an hour on a wrong road he had returned to the market town, called at the police station, and promptly been offered an escort.

The constable who had accompanied him smiled a little smugly.

'Five of our men are watching, sir, but you won't catch sight of one of them.'

'That's fine,' said Beresford.

'The Inspector has given each of them a position,' the policeman went on. 'I'll be relieving one of them at six o'clock, that's why I was at the station.'

He led the way to a stile, then walked along a footpath bordering the grounds of The Lees towards the woods where the shabby little man had been seen.

'My position is just inside a clearing at the end of the fence, sir,' said the policeman importantly. 'You can see the side of the house from there, but you can't be seen.'

He was the first to go forward, consequently Beresford did not see anything for some seconds, but he heard the exclamation of horror.

'What's the trouble?' he asked quickly.

His companion did not answer, and Beresford saw that he was leaning over the body of a man, half hidden by bracken and leaves. The policeman turned, a savage note in his voice.

'He's dead.'

'Steady on,' said Beresford quickly. 'They're using a knock-out drug in this game, and—'

He broke off as the other stood aside to enable him to see

the outstretched body. There was no question of a drug or of recovery; this man's throat had been cut.

Beresford tightened his lips, as he turned about.

'Can you drive?'

'Yes, sir.'

'Go back to Wimborne, and get more men at once. We're going to need them, if we're not too late.'

CHAPTER SIXTEEN

EMPTY HOUSE?

Beresford heard his car start off as he reached the front of The Lees. He stepped to a window beside the porch. It was closed, but the light was good enough to show him that it was not latched. He could not prise it up with his fingers, but was able to get enough purchase with his pen-knife.

The window squeaked loudly as he pushed it up.

He waited for a moment, but there was no further sound.

He stepped through into the dining-room.

As he moved there was a macabre thought in his mind, and he found it difficult to rid himself of it. One policeman had been murdered, but five should have been waiting and watching. Were all five dead? Did the woods and the hedges about The Lees hide their bodies?

He opened the door leading to the hall.

There was no sound, but Beresford told himself that it was not surprising; few households would be up so early. He did not know what staff arrangements Hennessy had. There could be one person here or a dozen.

He half expected to find Hennessy dead.

No one was in the downstairs rooms, and in the uncanny silence Beresford went upstairs. He had his revolver in his hand, cocked and ready for action. He wished he were not alone, and above all, that Dawlish was with him.

The study, and the bedrooms on the first floor, were empty. In one of them the bed was tumbled as if it had been slept in. He felt the sheets; they were quite cold.

'He hasn't been here in the last half-hour,' said Beresford softly. 'It's Hennessy's room, for a fortune.'

He went up a narrow flight of stairs to the top floor. There were three bedrooms there, and a box-room. Two of the bedrooms were obviously in regular use, but there was no sign of the occupants.

A creak sounded behind Beresford.

He swung round, and thought he saw a movement by the door. He fired, the bullet thudded into the opposite wall; but there was no further sound.

Cautiously he stepped into the passage. He saw no one, and heard nothing.

'I'm getting jittery,' he said aloud. 'It won't do.'

He looked up at a square patch in the ceiling. It was a loft entrance, with a hatch-cover across it. He hesitated, waiting in utter silence, apprehensive of what he could neither see nor hear.

'The police will be at least another half-hour,' he mused slowly. 'I wonder if I ought to look downstairs again? And whether there's a cellar?' He stepped to the head of the stairs, and then looked round. Glancing upwards, the dark patch of the loft entrance looked a little out of place. Against one side there was a triangle of white. He frowned, and went forward slowly.

Tall though he was he could not reach the hatch. He fetched a chair from the nearest bedroom, stood on it unsteadily, and then pushed the cover upwards. The triangle of white grew larger. He pulled at it, and a moment later was staring at a woman's handkerchief.

His lips tightened.

He saw initials worked on one corner, and uttered them aloud, his heart beating fast.

'E.J.T., by God! Elvira-dash-Templeton.' A pause, and then: 'What the hell am I waiting for?'

He stuffed the handkerchief into his pocket and pushed at the cover, moving it to one side without much trouble. Hauling his body up and through, he found himself gazing into darkness. He took his torch from his pocket and shone it, but the battery was low and it revealed only packing cases and oddments of furniture. He turned the light towards the sides of the entrance, and saw an electric switch.

He pressed it down.

A bright light shone on a cistern and something beyond it.

Beresford said in a dazed voice: 'My God! *Four of them!*'

For a split-second he stood still, then hurried forward. He saw a girl and three men lying bound and gagged. One of the men had managed to loosen his gag and stared up wildly.

'Who are you?'

'From Dawlish,' said Beresford. He did not need to ask the man his name, for he recognised Hennessy from Dawlish's description.

'For God's sake help me!' gasped Hennessy. 'We can't have much longer.'

Beresford took a knife out of his pocket and cut through the cord binding the other's wrists.

'Now my ankles, I must get out of here!'

'What's the hurry?' demanded Beresford.

'You damned fool, don't waste time talking! The place will be blown up!'

Beresford stared at the pale face and bright eyes, recognising an almost hysterical fear. He turned to the girl, saying harshly:

'How do you know?'

'Unfasten my ankles!' gasped Hennessy. 'I saw them put the explosive in the room beneath this, and there's another lot in the lounge. I must get away!'

'Untie your own ankles,' said Beresford roughly.

His knife severed the cords binding the girl. He then cut the bonds of the two men, one of whom he imagined to be Rennett.

None was conscious.

Hennessy's cords fell away. Gasping, the man staggered to his feet. He reached the exit, then drew back. 'I can't get down there, you must help me!'

'You'll get down,' said Beresford.

His contempt for the man had flared into acute anger, and he pushed past him, reached the hole, and lowered Elvira through it. He was able to keep a hold on her wrists until her feet touched the floor beneath. He let her go, then, and turned back for the men.

Hennessy stared at him, appearing to realise that he would get no further help. Breathing convulsively, he reached the hole and began to lower himself. When Beresford reached the side again the man was on his feet and running for the stairs.

'Take the girl!' roared Beresford. 'Take—'

He stopped abruptly, realising that it was useless, that Hennessy was in deathly fear of his life and that nothing could be done to make him change his tactics. Beresford dropped the first man through then returned for the other.

The brooding sense of urgency remained. He thought:

'The brute's right, the place is going up. If the T.N.T.'s in the lounge and the back of the house, the nearer we are to the front the better. I wonder what the odds are?' He felt a throbbing in his head as he raised the last man, and dragged him to the edge.

Lowering himself first, he stretched up and gripped the other's feet, pulling him down to the landing.

There was the sound of a banging door, and he thought he heard footsteps outside.

Tight-lipped, he raised the girl to his shoulder, held her there with one arm, then gripped the collar of Rennett's coat and dragged him to the stairs. Going down was not easy, and there was sweat on his forehead when he went back for the third man. He hurried then, his ears cocked for the slightest sound, expecting to hear the roar at any moment. His heart was thumping as he repeated the process down the main staircase. The front door was only a few yards away from the bottom step. He hurried through it with the girl in his arms, dropping her on the grass verge of the drive, and returning at a run for the men. He did not try to carry them, but dragged one at a time, his fore-head dripping sweat, veins standing out on his neck and arms.

He was half-way out of the porch with the last man when the explosion came.

There was a roar and a trembling; and then chaos. Walls bulged and split open, bricks and plaster flew in all directions. He felt debris falling on him, something heavy struck his back and made him gasp. Dust rose in great clouds, choking him. He heard the rumbling, going on and on but after a while grew aware that nothing more was falling.

He tried to move, but could not; whatever had struck his back was pinning him down.

And he was afraid, lest another explosion came.

CHAPTER SEVENTEEN

A SHOCK FOR ROBBIE

Inspector Medway of the Wimborne Police heard the explosion when he was two miles away from The Lees. A moment later he saw the cloud of dust and smoke rising up, and he exclaimed:

'That's Hennessy's house!'

A policeman next to him said:

'The gentleman said he was going in, sir.'

'Tread on it,' said Medway urgently.

In the tonneau of the police car were two other men, and on the road behind, two laden cars maintained the speed of the first. In five minutes Medway was jumping to the ground. He saw the girl and the body of a man, lying on the verge.

The front walls of The Lees had withstood the explosion fairly well, although piles of debris filled the doorway.

Medway and two policemen reached the porch.

They could see the hand of a man sticking through the rubble.

Medway summoned others hurriedly. From the toolshed they found spades and forks, and axes, and with these they worked swiftly.

In twenty minutes the beam which pinned Beresford down was raised, and the big man crawled out.

His face was bleeding, and he was covered with dust. One eye was closed up, and he held one hand tightly against his side.

He gasped:

'Another fellow. Be careful. More of the stuff.'

He staggered away, helped by one of the policemen. By then several people had arrived from nearby cottages, and Beresford, Rennett, and the girl were put into cars and taken to the nearest house.

In half an hour, Medway had the third man free. He did not recognise him, but a quick examination suggested that the man was not badly hurt.

A sergeant said: 'They've come out of it well, sir.'

'Yes,' said Medway. 'We'd better start looking for our own fellows.' The last of the rescued men taken to the nearest house, Medway joined in the search.

In twenty minutes he had the full total. Of the five policemen, two were dead, but the others were in much the same condition as Dawlish had been when found in the New Forest.

Medway superintended the work of clearing the house for a thorough inspection, until relieved. Then he went to see Beresford. When he reached the house where the victims had been taken he learned that Rennett and the second man had been taken into the local hospital, but that Beresford and the girl were conscious.

Beresford appeared, his right eye discoloured, his cheeks covered with crosses of sticking-plaster.

In spite of that he essayed a grin.

'Dawlish told me about you,' he said. 'How did things go? Your men, I mean?'

Medway told him quietly.

'So it could have been worse,' said Beresford. He scowled

as he went on: 'That skunk Hennessy could have helped to get them away and we'd have been safe enough. Instead of that he just scuttled off. Where is he?'

'I don't know,' said Medway slowly.

'You don't—' Beresford paused. 'Do you mean you haven't seen him?'

'I haven't,' said Medway grimly. 'But it won't be long before I do.'

In that Medway proved an optimist, for although he telephoned to his headquarters and arranged for a general call to be put out immediately, Hennessy was not found that day.

Many other things happened.

Rennett was not on the danger list, but the second man proved to be worse than expected. Elvira was sent to London for an interview with Dawlish. Beresford escorted her, while for safety's sake a police car followed them as far as the Great West Road, where a car from Scotland Yard took over.

Beresford soon gave up trying to keep a conversation going. As he drove on he ruminated that although they had stopped at Basingstoke for coffee, and had been together for nearly four hours, the girl had said nothing except how she and Rennett had left their house.

He turned the car into Jermyn Street, braked, and looked about him, seeing two of Trivett's men on the other side of the road.

Their arrival had been observed, for the door of the flat opened and Robbie Graham appeared. He stared at Elvira, and then looked at Beresford with an uncertain smile.

'All here and all safe,' reported Beresford. 'How's Pat?'

'Come and see for yourself,' called Dawlish from inside.

'Well I'm damned!' exclaimed Beresford. 'Well, well, well! So you're all in one piece, and you can move about. Pat, I'm darned glad to see you!'

'I'm not so sorry to see you,' said Dawlish. 'Medway has been on the phone, and told me a thing or two.'

'Don't believe half what he says,' said Beresford awkwardly. 'There's no news of Hennessy yet, I suppose?'

Dawlish shook his head.

'I should have hobbled the beggar,' mused Beresford. 'He deserved anything that happened to him. D'you know, Pat, as soon as he was free he legged it. I thought he'd lend a hand with the others, but oh dear no! Number 1 first and foremost with Mr. Hennessy. Well, I've brought the talkative lady,' he added, grinning at Elvira. 'What's more, her uncle has given her permission to tell all she knows, so we *might* hear something.' He looked across to the kitchen. 'Where's Fel?'

'Getting lunch ready,' said Dawlish. 'Tony is helping her. We're going to be crowded,' he added. 'Tim's coming up from Bournemouth, there wasn't much point in him staying there.' He eyed Elvira evenly, and added: 'You believe in asking for trouble, don't you?'

Elvira flushed.

'When do you want me to tell you what I know?'

'After lunch,' said Dawlish, 'if that's all right with you.'

'Damn it, it might be important!' exclaimed Robbie.

'It's been unknown for so long that another hour's delay won't do any harm,' said Dawlish.

Ten minutes later they were all sitting down to lunch. The meal passed quietly enough. As the meal wore on, comments grew fewer. Dawlish contributed little to the conversation, and there was an atmosphere of strain about the flat. Once or twice Elvira looked across at Dawlish, and Felicity noticed that her expression was tense and strained.

Suddenly she pushed her chair back, rounded the table, and went blindly into the other room. Felicity started to follow her, but Dawlish caught at her arm.

'Leave her,' he said.

'Are you being deliberately cruel?' Felicity asked.

Dawlish gave a humourless smile.

'If letting Elvira know that I don't approve of what she's done is being cruel, I suppose so.'

'Damn it!' exclaimed Robbie hotly. 'What is the point of it? Beresford says that she arranged with her uncle to tell you everything she can. What more do you want!'

'You're very anxious to champion Elvira, aren't you?' said Dawlish mildly.

'I'm only doing what any decent fellow would do,' snapped Robbie. 'I think you're a damned sight too high-and-mighty over some things, Dawlish. I'm getting tired of it.'

Glaring at Dawlish, he hurried in Elvira's wake, banging the door behind him.

Thoughtfully Dawlish rubbed his nose. 'It seems that I'm not popular,' he commented.

'Well, you did rather ask for it, Pat,' agreed Tony Grayling slowly.

'What is going on in that little mind of yours, Pat?' interjected Ted quietly.

Dawlish shrugged.

'A roundabout of questions, and it's time some of them were answered. Now the first one is—why was Robbie met at Liverpool, and thereafterwards attacked? There's another: why did Robbie choose to pour out his troubles to me? We are no more than acquaintances, you know, or we weren't until this affair.'

Tony stared at him.

'You're not suspecting *Robbie* of complicity?'

'Let's say I'm keeping an open mind,' said Dawlish, and pointedly changed the subject. 'Come on, let's do justice to Fel's cooking.'

He smiled at Felicity, who eyed him thoughtfully. She did not voice her feelings, but it was easy to see that like Tony and, to a lesser degree Ted and Tim, she was wondering whether his attitude was necessary. There was much sympathy in the air for Elvira; and, she knew that, normally, Dawlish too would have felt the same. Instead he had made a difficult position for the girl even more trying.

The telephone rang abruptly.

Dawlish opened the lounge door as the ringing finished. The others saw Robbie move away quickly from Elvira's side. Both of them looked startled at Dawlish's appearance.

'Sorry. That call will be for me, I expect.'

Dawlish lifted the receiver, and heard Trivett's voice.

'Hallo, Bill,' he said. 'I've been waiting to hear from you. What's the news?' He pulled a chair up and sat down, watched by the couple in the room and the quartette sitting round the dining-table.

'We haven't lost any time,' said the Yard man with more than a trace of satisfaction. 'Whitehead asked us to check up on the four people you haven't visited yet—Train, Rosstein, Cornwallis, and Mrs. Benn.'

'Yes,' said Dawlish.

'We've asked them all whether they know Hennessy, Pollittzer, Mrs. Arthurson, and Rennett,' said Trivett. 'They do. The reaction in three cases was normal enough, but Rosstein seemed nervous and annoyed at the question. You might be well-advised to look him up, Pat.'

'I'll have him looked up, anyhow,' Dawlish assured him. 'So

they're all acquaintances. You didn't happen to find out whether they've moved away from the Dorset area lately, did you?'

'I did,' said Trivett. 'Rosstein has a country cottage near Lyme Regis but his regular home is at Hampstead. Train has always lived in Fulham but has spent a great deal of time in Dorset as a guest of the real Dr. Pollittzer; he's an archaeologist, an amateur but very keen. Cornwallis lived near Dorchester until two years ago when business brought him to Little Granley, and Mrs. Benn was at one time Dr. Pollittzer's housekeeper. She's an old woman, rather weak-minded, I'd say.'

'Good man,' said Dawlish. 'That's all we wanted. I'll let you know if anything crops up. 'Bye for the time being.'

Dawlish replaced the receiver and stood for a moment looking at Robbie Graham and Elvira. From the other room there was silence; in fact the whole flat was very quiet. A ruminative smile on Dawlish's face faded, and he turned his gaze towards Robbie.

'Something new keeps cropping up,' said Dawlish slowly. 'I had an interesting piece of information then. About you,' he added mendaciously, and his expression hardened.

'About *me!*' exclaimed Robbie.

'That's right,' said Dawlish. 'About you, Robbie. Isn't it time you told me the whole truth?' He stepped forward, and Robbie backed away, his face ludicrous in amazement. 'Isn't it time, for instance, that you told me how long you've known Elvira?'

From the other room there came a long, low whistle of astonishment.

CHAPTER EIGHTEEN

ELVIRA BECOMES TALKATIVE

Robbie cleared his throat nervously.

'What—what are you talking about?' he muttered.

'There'll be no more hedging,' snapped Dawlish. 'Either the two of you will tell the whole truth, or you'll stay in jail until the affair's over.'

'You—you must be crazy!' gasped Robbie.

Dawlish drew a deep breath, and then said harshly:

'What kind of affair do you think this is? What gives you the idea that you can let your own petty little interests take precedence over things that really matter? How long are you going to forget that there's a war on? Out with it! How long have you known Elvira?'

Into a short, tense pause, Elvira said:

'For over two years, Captain Dawlish.'

Dawlish's expression relaxed.

'That's better,' he said. 'Robbie, you were met at Liverpool by Bateson, and we always wondered why that was. How the fact that you were on your ship was learned I don't know yet, but I do know why you were met.'

Robbie said nothing.

'It's just dawned on me,' admitted Dawlish. He turned to the girl. 'Robbie was wanted because he knew you, your uncle, Pollittzer and all the others. As obviously, you had written to him and told him something of what was happening, and he jumped at the chance to come over here. Once here, he saw how things were going and didn't like the look of them. He knew what your uncle was doing, so he didn't want to go to the police. It wouldn't surprise me,' added Dawlish quietly, 'if you prevailed on him not to, Elvira.'

'I did,' Elvira admitted.

'Well, our knowledge is growing. You were worried about what would happen if the police learned that you were planted in Hennessy's house, and you didn't think they would be long finding what your uncle was after. Isn't that right?'

She nodded.

'So Robbie was sworn to silence,' continued Dawlish slowly. 'But the other side knew that he'd been to see you, guessed why he was so quick to visit you, and made further attempts to kill him. That worried him. He knew that you and your uncle had been threatened, and believed you were in danger. So,' said Dawlish, 'he thought up a good one. He kept his word to you, Elvira, and didn't go to the police, but he salved his conscience by telling me the story and hoping that I'd be interested. Did you know that?'

'He's just told me so,' said Elvira. 'But how did you learn all this?'

Dawlish shrugged. 'When you work things out the usual solution is the simple one, and the simple one in this case is that Robbie was in danger for precisely the same reason as the rest of you. I had wondered whether Robbie knew you as well as the others, and so the show-down at lunch was more or less planned.'

Robbie dug his hands deep in his pockets.

'I didn't dream you'd cotton on to it, Dawlish. I—oh, I suppose I was a pretty damned fool, but what else could I do? You're right enough. I've read a lot about you, and I followed you into the Carilon the other night in the hope of having a chat. I suppose it seems pretty crazy, but—' He broke off, helplessly.

Elvira said awkwardly:

'My uncle and I didn't tell you all the truth the other night, you know that now.'

'I was afraid of it,' admitted Dawlish.

'It was so difficult,' said Elvira quickly. 'The truth isn't credible in some ways.' She paused, then went on sharply: 'The real trouble is about the jewels. My uncle was suspected of stealing them. He was questioned by the police in Singapore, and they weren't satisfied that he was innocent. He'd been seen near the scene of the robbery, you see. I don't think the English Police know that he's suspect, but he's afraid that sooner or later something will happen, and he wants to make sure about Hennessy. So I took the job, to try to find what I could.' She paused again, and then added intently: 'Does that seem more reasonable?'

Dawlish said quietly: 'It offers a sound enough reason for you taking the job, yes, and for wanting to keep quiet about it. But let's not hedge, Elvira, it isn't going to help us. The case against your uncle was pretty strong, wasn't it?'

After a few seconds, Elvira said:

'Yes, it was. The bags in which the jewels had been kept were found on board Uncle's ship. The Singapore Police believed he threw the gems overboard.'

'I see,' said Dawlish. 'And you told Robbie all this?'

'Yes, of course.'

Robbie broke in quietly:

'Vi was with me when I was first shot at. We had a council of war, and I thought of you. I'd seen you in London on my way from Liverpool, so I decided to try to get you interested. But I'd no idea that there was anything bigger behind it than jewels.'

'Is there anything bigger?' asked Elvira.

Dawlish eyed her thoughtfully.

'Much bigger. At the same time as the jewels were stolen papers were stolen from Singapore of much greater importance, containing military information.' He lit a cigarette and flicked the match into the fireplace. 'Now, we've got two more things to work at. First, what did you learn about Hennessy? Your uncle hinted at a great deal. And second, what happened at The Lees?'

By then the company was sitting about the lounge, and the atmosphere was much lighter. Felicity suggested tea, and Elvira offered to help her. The men were left alone for ten minutes. Dawlish knew well that Felicity had manoeuvred this deliberately. Robbie was not slow in taking advantage of it. He repeated much of what he had already said, but made it clear that his chief anxiety was for Elvira. He had been anxious to help her all he could, and been worried when she had hinted at trouble in her letters. He had known about the suspicions against Rennett before he had left for Libya, and the fact that the old sailor had been pushed over the edge of the cliff at Westbourne, and narrowly escaped death.

Towards the end of his story, Robbie said slowly:

'I suppose I ought to be court-martialled for this, Dawlish. But honestly—'

'Let's forget it,' said Dawlish. 'We've got the whole truth now, I think. I don't see that it would have made much difference had I known earlier,' he added generously. 'My approach to the affair might have been different, but not necessarily more effective. The thing that I haven't fathomed yet is why so many people are on Kohn's books.'

'Kohn?'

Dawlish explained as much as was necessary of the man in black.

Robbie said helplessly: 'I just don't know anything about the others. Rennett doesn't either, as far as I know.'

The girls came in then, with tea.

Dawlish took a cup from Elvira.

'Did you ever learn why Hennessy went abroad?' he asked.

'Yes. Before he retired he was a Far Eastern representative of Lex Oils,' Elvira told him. 'They asked him to go out and inspect the wells in which it has an interest. There was a lot of correspondence, and the Lex people said they could arrange the Government permit, but that it would be wise for him not to disclose his main purpose.'

'Lex Oils,' said Dawlish reflectively. 'They're quite a small company, aren't they?'

'I don't know much about them,' admitted Elvira.

'We'll find out.' Dawlish stepped to the telephone and dialled Scotland Yard. Trivett was in his room. Dawlish asked him whether he knew anything of Lex Oils, and whether he would try to find out more.

'They're shaky,' said Trivett slowly. 'There are rumours of them going into liquidation in the City. I'll see what I can find out.'

He rang off, and Elvira said quietly:

'You don't lose time, do you?'

'There isn't any to lose,' said Dawlish. 'What else do you know?'

Elvira sipped her tea before going on.

'Well—I don't know that this helps, but Hennessy had a number of visitors, including Dr. Pollittzer, Mrs. Arthurson, and all the people you mentioned when you telephoned

Scotland Yard first. Rosstein, Cornwallis, Train, and that funny little Mrs. Benn.'

Dawlish said softly:

'Did he, by Jove!'

Elvira went on: 'The thing I thought rather odd was that Mrs. Arthurson visited Hennessy. It was public gossip that they'd quarrelled because he was a pacifist, and opposed to the war. She always came after dark, and entered with a key.'

'Yes, that's odd all right,' said Dawlish. 'But it's getting clearer. With The Lees blown up, and the papers destroyed or taken away, there are a lot of things we wouldn't have discovered but for you.' He smiled. 'On the whole I think we're doing well, but there's one other thing. What possessed you and your uncle to sneak away last night and visit Hennessy?'

Elvira hesitated, and then said slowly:

'Hennessy telephoned Uncle, and said that he wanted to see him. He said that it was urgent and important. We didn't know what to do at first, but—well, you've met Uncle, you can imagine what he said when I advised him not to go.'

'Yes,' said Dawlish, 'your uncle is certainly an impetuous man. So Hennessy got you there as simply as that?'

Elvira leant forward eagerly. 'He thought there was a chance that Hennessy was going to make some kind of an admission, or to make amends somehow or other. It was all rather vague, but if you were as absolutely honest as Uncle, and had that suspicion hanging over you, you'd probably have felt much the same.'

'Hum,' said Dawlish. 'Well just one other thing, Elvira. The evening before, your uncle was tied to his bed.'

'Some days he's better than others,' Elvira told him. 'If he really sets himself to it he can get about, though with a good deal of pain. One of my chief difficulties has been keeping him in bed.'

'And that's the lot?' asked Dawlish.

'That's the lot,' declared Elvira. She paused, then added: 'Does it help?'

'Our first problem is completely solved,' said Dawlish with confidence. 'Hennessy was the pivot around which the people on Bateson's list worked. We know that you were attacked bcause you might have stumbled across some fact which would give the whole show away—that's why they didn't stop at trying to scare Robbie, but tried to kill him. I think we can safely say,' he added with a smile, 'that Hennessy was afraid that your uncle would discover something, and so they tried to kill him on the cliff.'

'I still don't see—' began Robbie.

'Hush, don't confess to it,' abjured Dawlish. 'Hennessy was an important executive of Lex Oils. He accepted a special mission during the war, although he was retired. He went out East and made contacts. The people in a position to know that, and to know just what he did, were the directors of Lex Oils, and possibly its principal shareholders.'

'You mean they're the people on the list?'

'Just that,' said Dawlish quietly.

Twenty minutes later the telephone rang. Trivett's voice, almost squeaking with excitement, came through at once.

'Pat, listen to me. The Chairman and Managing Director of Lex Oils is Jacob Rosstein, the other directors are the people on your list, with the exception of Rennett, who has nothing to do with the company. Hennessy joined the board after retiring from an executive position, and went abroad earlier in the war on a special mission. Hennessy was in a position to make contact with all the pro-Japanese elements there. Do you see what that means?'

'Yes,' said Dawlish quickly. 'It means that we want Hennessy badly. Is there any word of him?'

'Not yet,' admitted Trivett, 'but we'll get him.'

'We've got to get him. Is Rosstein being watched?'

'Of course, by two men.'

'Good. Send word to your fellows that I'll be along soon. The quicker I see the gentlemen the better.'

Dawlish replaced the receiver and turned to the others, giving them a quick *resume* of the news. He arranged for Elvira and Felicity to stay at the flat, and for Tim Jeremy to keep them company.

Robbie was obviously so anxious to make some kind of amends that Dawlish had not the heart to leave him behind. He felt that there was danger for Elvira, and therefore wanted one of the men at the flat, but he felt even more the urgency of seeing Rosstein.

He did not, of course, know that at that moment Rosstein was looking across his desk into Hennessy's handsome face, and saying harshly:

'You've got to get away, can't you see that? The police are on to me, they might search the place at any time. You've got to clear out!'

Hennessy's voice rang high.

'They won't search it until tonight, and I'm not moving until it's dark. No one knows I'm here, and—'

He broke off abruptly, seeing Rosstein glance towards the door, his eyes widening. Hennessy swung round, then half-rose from his chair.

'I thought I would find you here,' said the man in black. 'Sit down, Hennessy. And you, Rosstein. I overheard your conversation,' he added, 'and found it most interesting. The police won't come themselves, I think, but Dawlish will. Supposing we make preparations to receive him?'

CHAPTER NINETEEN

MR. ROSSTEIN IS FRIGHTENED

There was a tense silence in Rosstein's study.

The Chairman and Managing Director of Lex Oils sat stiffly in his chair, looking at the man in black. Hennessy did not move, until the little man with the nut-cracker face following his master grinned at him.

'What's the matter, scared?' he demanded.

'Quiet,' said the man in black, 'and be careful with that gun.'

Rosstein's face turned a greyish colour. His heavy jowl and full cheeks quivered a little; there was little doubt that he was a badly frightened man.

'What—what are you doing here?' he muttered. 'Kohn, you must be crazy!'

'Not crazy,' said Kohn, 'but very careful. On your own admission the police have been making inquiries. I have little doubt that Dawlish inspired them. We certainly need a reception committee for Dawlish, and any of his friends he thinks to bring with him.'

Rosstein gasped: 'But the police are outside, I saw them! They know you're here.'

'They saw me arrive,' amended Kohn, 'and they will see me go out. Or they will think that. Actually our mutual friend Hennessy will go in my place.'

Hennessy said nothing.

'My chauffeur is waiting at the car,' said Kohn. 'Catten was lying on the floor, and was hidden even from the police, so they will not know that he is here with me.' He took off his hat and coat, and held them towards Hennessy. 'Put them on.'

Hennessy obeyed without arguing.

Rosstein sat at his desk, his hands resting in front of him, staring into Kohn's eyes. The nut-cracker man, Catten, took Hennessy downstairs.

When Catten returned, Rosstein said in a strangled voice:

'You're losing your senses, Kohn. If Dawlish comes he'll catch you here. I can bluff him, but you can't.'

Kohn said: 'That is a matter of opinion. Your opinion, not mine.' He smiled mirthlessly. 'I will tell you just what our arrangements are,' he went on. 'They are simple enough.'

Kohn talked for five minutes. As he spoke something of Rosstein's fears evaporated, and once or twice he laughed.

Dawlish stopped the Lagonda at the end of Elm Street, and looked along the tree-lined avenue.

The dashboard clock pointed to three-forty-five.

'I don't see the police,' said Tony Grayling.

'We shouldn't be able to,' said Dawlish. 'Here are the others, we're all set.'

Ted Beresford and Robbie Graham climbed from the car which had turned the corner as Dawlish spoke, and the four-some met on the pavement. None of them knew which was Lintara, the home of Jacob Rosstein.

Robbie was despatched to locate the house. He went off

eagerly, happy at the thought of any kind of action. As Dawlish watched him go, Beresford said:

'Are you still wondering if you've heard everything from him, Pat?'

'Ye-es,' admitted Dawlish. 'I think we have, but one can never be absolutely sure.' He shrugged. 'Rosstein may be expecting us,' he added, 'the police questions will have warned him.'

'How are we tackling him?' asked Ted.

'Robbie and I go in, you and Tony stay out here. Give me twenty minutes, and if you've heard nothing by then yell for the police and come to the house without losing time.'

Ted nodded, satisfied.

Tony Grayling looked uncertain.

'Pat, if you seriously think there's a possibility that Robbie's in this, is it safe to take him in with you?'

'I can't think of a better way of keeping an eye on him.'

Tony nodded, smiling a little.

'The more I think of it, the more sure I am that Rosstein will expect us,' Dawlish went on. 'If he does, and he's a party to the game, we're going to have a warm welcome. After the show at The Lees we know that these beggars like to strike at the watchers, so you two be careful.'

He walked along to join Robbie, gazing idly at two workmen replacing the cover of a manhole. Tony Grayling eyed Ted helplessly.

'Does he always take these chances?'

'Always,' admitted Beresford. 'The trouble is that he keeps getting new ideas. The Lord knows what he expects now, but it's something pretty hot.'

They watched Dawlish and Robbie disappear into one of the driveways, and followed leisurely.

Lintara, the home of Jacob Rosstein, was not remarkable for

its architectural beauty. It was a square, solid residence, built of red brick. The effect was ugly. The drive showed the marks of tyres, and Dawlish glanced at them curiously.

'Someone's been here recently. I wonder who it was?' He did not invite suggestions, but put a finger on the bell-push and waited.

A middle-aged man opened the door.

'Good afternoon,' said Dawlish. 'Is Mr. Rosstein in?'

'I think so, sir.'

'Tell him that Captain Dawlish and Lieutenant Graham would like a word with him, will you?'

'Yes, sir. May I state your business?'

'It concerns Mr. Hennessy,' said Dawlish promptly.

The man bowed and stood aside. Dawlish and Graham entered an indifferently furnished hall, prepared to wait.

'It's not much of a place,' commented Robbie.

'Rosstein's probably not much of a man,' said Dawlish.

Robbie grinned. 'What are you going to say to the chap when you see him?'

Before Dawlish could answer, the manservant returned, and asked them to follow him. He was light-footed, soft-moving, and over-polite. Dawlish frowned at his back as they walked up the stairs, feeling a peculiar sense of tension.

The man reached a square landing, and approached a door which was standing ajar.

'This way, gentlemen, please.'

Jacob Rosstein was sitting behind his desk. As they entered he ostentatiously blotted something he had been writing, and stood up, extending a plump hand, on which a diamond ring sparkled.

A warning reared up in Dawlish's mind.

The smile was false; everything about Rosstein oozed

geniality when it should have shown uncertainty, perhaps puzzlement. This was the man who had shown unfavourable reaction to police questions, but was now smiling and affable, as though he had no anxieties and no fears.

'Sit down, sit down, gentlemen. I'm very glad to see you, very glad indeed.' He beamed. 'Cigars?' He pushed a box across his desk. 'Now, what can I do for you?'

'You don't seem particularly surprised to see us,' said Dawlish drily.

'That's right, that's dead right!' exclaimed Rosstein. 'It takes a lot to surprise me, and I've heard a thing or two about *you*, Captain.' He smiled widely.

Dawlish said easily: 'And from whom have you done that?'

'Well, Hennessy, of course!' Rosstein chuckled at the astonishment on Robbie's face, and went on heartily: 'Is that a surprise? Hennessy came to see me last night, and again this morning. Ever seen a frightened rabbit, Captain? That's Hennessy! Never seen a man so scared in all my life.'

'Is that so?' asked Dawlish.

'You don't need telling, I bet!' Rosstein laughed again. 'He told me about the trouble he had, and how that friend of yours came along just in time, But mind you—' Rosstein stopped smiling, and frowned as if deeply concerned. 'Hennessy didn't come out of that very well, he was too scared. I can imagine what *you* think about him, Captain.'

Dawlish thought: He's talking to gain time.

The impression of danger which he had felt on entering the house grew stronger. Aloud he said quietly:

'Is Hennessy still here?'

'Lord love you, no! He's gone. I soon had him out of here,' said Rosstein heartily. 'I knew the police would be looking for him, and I didn't want any trouble with them until I'd seen you.'

'I don't remember making an appointment.'

Rosstein stared, then opened his mouth and roared with laughter.

'An appointment! That's good! Ha-ha-ha!' He grew sober abruptly, too abruptly, and leaned forward. 'Now I'm not a fool, Captain Dawlish, and after what I'd heard I realised you would soon be wanting to know what I could tell you about Hennessy. Well, it's plenty, but I don't know whether it will help you.' He glanced at his wrist-watch, licked his lips, and went on: 'Now we don't want to waste time, do we? Supposing I tell you what I can, and then you can form your own opinion. That's fair.'

Dawlish crossed his legs and said lightly:

'It's fair, yes. Or it would be if I believed a word of what you're saying. The trouble is, I don't. What time's zero hour?'

Rosstein gaped at him.

'What time's zero hour,' repeated Dawlish. 'You wouldn't try the same trick twice, and blow this place up like you did The Lees. Or would you?' he added conversationally, and slid his revolver from its holster.

There was a moment of absolute silence before Rosstein gasped: 'I don't know what you're talking about!'

'Now, come,' said Dawlish. 'You know as well as I do. Did Hennessy arrange the trick with you, or was it Kohn?'

'T-ttrick!' exclaimed Rosstein in a strangled voice. 'W-what trick?'

'The one that isn't going to work,' said Dawlish patiently. 'Robbie, have a look at the door, will you, and see whether anyone is in the passage.'

A little vein was moving in and out of Rosstein's throat.

'C-Captain, what are you talking about? I don't—I don't understand you!'

From the door Robbie said: 'The passage is empty.'

'All right, thanks,' said Dawlish. 'Stay there for a moment. Rosstein—' He leaned forward, and his gun was only a few inches from Rosstein's chest. *What time is zero hour?*

The man half rose from his chair, his face suffused to a deep red, the vein beating more quickly.

'You've got me all wrong, Dawlish! Put that gun away! I—'

Rosstein stumbled backwards, his chair fell and he crashed down. Dawlish rounded the desk and hauled the man up.

'Talk while you've the chance!' he said harshly. 'What's going to happen here?'

'N-nothing! Nothing, you're mad, you can't act like this!' Rosstein plucked ineffectually at Dawlish's wrists.

'The police are outside,' Dawlish went on, 'so are my friends. If the police get you you'll stand a normal trial, but if I take you away you'll get treatment you don't expect. Come on, what's going to happen here?' He was intent only on one thing; frightening the man. He was succeeding.

'Let me go! gasped Rosstein.

Dawlish let him go, and the man staggered back against the wall. He stared at Dawlish for a moment, then glanced at his watch. Dawlish saw that it wanted a few minutes to half past four.

Rosstein's lips worked, and he muttered:

'I—I've got—I've got an appointment soon, I can't stay here any longer.'

Dawlish eyed him grimly, the gun poking towards the man's chest.

'That's one of the weakest efforts I've ever heard, Rosstein. So you had to get out of this room at half past four, did you? You had to keep me here until then and then slide off? Listen to me. I'm staying here, and so are you, until I know what's coming.'

Rosstein turned colour.

'You—you can't keep me here.' He had been frightened enough when Kohn had talked to him, but now he was terrified. 'You can't keep me here, Dawlish!'

'We're staying,' said Dawlish.

'Oh my God!' gasped Rosstein. There was froth at the corners of his lips and terror in his eyes. 'Dawlish, get away from here! Get away, get away! We mustn't stay, we've only got a couple of minutes!'

'That's ample time,' said Dawlish equably.

'You're mad! You know what happened at The Lees. This place is going up, too, don't you understand? Let me go, let me get out!'

Dawlish said: 'I wonder if it could be true.'

'Of course it's true!' gasped Rosstein. 'I saw them put the explosive downstairs, I saw them!' He made a break for freedom, and rushed to the door.

Robbie turned to face him, but Dawlish called:

'All right, Robbie, let him pass.'

Rosstein flew past him, and down the stairs. His footsteps thudded heavily, while Robbie stared in stupefaction at Dawlish, and gasped:

'You heard what he said!'

'Ye-es,' said Dawlish. 'But I didn't believe him, Robbie. Kohn wouldn't do it twice in exactly the same way. Remember what Ted told us of Hennessy's fears? Rosstein used almost the same words. Something's coming, but I don't think it's coming to the house, it's smarter than that.'

'But su-supposing it does?' stammered Robbie.

'It'll be too bad,' said Dawlish. 'Robbie, they would know that Rosstein would crack. They would know I was expecting some kind of a trick. They would reckon on Rosstein behaving as he has done, on running out of the house. Of course they would, it's obvious. The next thing that's obvious is that we would follow him. My God! Those workmen!'

He turned about in sudden urgency, cracked his elbow through the window, and glimpsed Ted Beresford in the grounds at the back of the house.

'Ted!' shouted Dawlish. 'Stay put! Don't move!'

He ran across the room, pushing past Robbie, and ran towards the landing window. The glass splintered. He saw the drive and Rosstein running along it wildly. Behind him was Tony Grayling in hot pursuit, and Dawlish shouted:

'Tony! Stay there!'

Tony turned on his heel.

Rosstein reached the drive gates and swung to the right. There was no doubt that he was terrified, that he believed the house would go up. In the tension which followed Dawlish glanced at his watch; it was twenty-five minutes to five.

It happened, then.

One moment Rosstein was running along the tree-lined avenue; the next there was a roar and a flash of flame. Rosstein just disappeared. Debris flew high into the air, as Grayling flung himself down. From all along the street came the explosion of shattered windows. There were flames, too.

Then the gateway of the house went up.

The second explosion roared against Dawlish's ear, shaking the house. Plaster fell about Dawlish's head and shoulders. There was a constant rumbling and echoing as the smoke billowed out in great clouds.

Dawlish said without expression:

'So Rosstein's gone, and we nearly went with him.' He turned abruptly and saw Robbie coming forward, covered with dust and plaster. Dawlish smiled a little grimly as he turned to the stairs. 'Let's get down to the others, old man, they might need help.'

In the grounds Ted Beresford was bending over Tony Grayling, who was protesting vigorously that he was all right; he looked a wreck. By then the street was filling with terrified people, some of whom were running towards the heath. Dawlish and Beresford hurried across the road, while from the garden of a house opposite a policeman came, shaky and uncertain.

'Were you on duty here?' asked Dawlish.

'Ye-es, sir. Superintendent Trivett stationed me.'

'Where's your companion?'

'He should be all right, he was at the back.'

'Good,' said Dawlish. 'Did you see anyone come along to the hydrant outside while you were watching?'

'Ye-es,' said the plainclothes man, staring. 'Two men came and were working for ten minutes or so.'

'They did the damage,' said Dawlish thoughtfully. 'The moment they saw Rosstein, they pressed the button.' He turned to Beresford. 'You know what that means, Ted?'

Beresford said slowly: 'That they were watching near by.'

'And may still be doing so,' said Dawlish. 'We aren't out of the wood yet.'

CHAPTER TWENTY

CONSULTATION AT AUDELEY STREET

In a very short time A.R.P. squads arrived, and the debris in Elm Street was cleared away. Water and gas mains were damaged, but not seriously, and workmen were soon busy putting them right. There were few whole windows left in the street, but little material damage had been done to the houses. The consternation which the explosions had caused died down.

In a room in Lintara the four men eyed one another.

Dawlish had telephoned Trivett within ten minutes of learning that no one but Rosstein had been seriously hurt, arranged for the police to try to trace two bogus workmen who had been busy outside Lintara. When he had finished, Robbie Graham said slowly:

'Had you any idea of what was going to happen, Pat?'

'No,' said Dawlish, 'though I was, of course, prepared for something. The obvious thing was an explosion, but I began to wonder after I'd seen Rosstein's state of nerves. If the house were to go up, I thought Rosstein wouldn't stay behind as a bait unless sure that he would be able to get out in time. I dismissed the idea of a time-fuse, for no one could be sure when I would arrive. But Rosstein's quick glances at his watch made it obvious that time was a factor.' Dawlish smiled. 'So I looked round for something else, making a guess that Kohn would want Rosstein killed as well as ourselves. It was obvious that he was not a man to be relied on, and even if he escaped the explosion he would be questioned by the police. From Kohn's point of view, Rosstein was much better out of the way.'

'Well, I'll be damned!' exclaimed Robbie.

Ted smiled: 'Beginning to see the way his mind goes round?'

'And round, and round,' said Dawlish. 'Now, what were the possibilities? I remembered the workmen at the hydrant, and realised that there was a method by which it could be worked. A press-button explosion was called for, the fuse laid somewhere handy but not too obvious. Under the pavement was a good idea. Kohn spent some time working that one out,' he added, 'and he did it darned well. A press as soon as Rosstein appeared to a mine in the street, then a second one, nearer the house, to catch those following him. Not a bad job.'

'Bad!' exclaimed Grayling. 'It's fiendish!'

'*We're* getting places,' said Dawlish. 'First Kohn wanted me alive but that was when he thought I might be convinced about the jewel motive. Now he knows I'm not, he's getting really worried.' He glanced out of the window. 'Ah, Trivett, and his invaluable aide, Munk!' he cried with satisfaction. 'They haven't lost any time.'

Trivett came into the lounge, smiled somewhat grimly. He listened in silence as Dawlish gave him a brief outline of what had happened, Detective-Sergeant Munk stood in the doorway. He had not yet made up his mind whether to approve of Dawlish, despite the three years and more of their association.

Trivett raised his hands helplessly as Dawlish finished.

'You're just not human,' he said. 'Oh, well, we'd better take things as they come. I'm doing all I can to find those workmen, Pat. Where shall I ring you if I have any luck?'

'The flat,' said Dawlish. 'If I'm not there one of the others will be. You'll go through this place pretty thoroughly, of course. And what about the headquarters of the Lex Company?'

'I've got that covered all right,' Trivett assured him. 'I'll have a report by tonight, I hope.'

Dawlish and his friends left the house soon afterwards. At the end of the street their cars were standing, covered with dust but not damaged. A crowd of sightseers were still milling about, avid for sensation. Dawlish eyed them thoughtfully.

'Kohn could hide a couple of men among that lot,' he suggested. 'Ted, will you and Tony drive round for half an hour, and keep an eye open for anyone who might folllow you? We've got to pick up a trail soon,' he added, and there was a touch of anxiety in his voice.

With Robbie beside him, Dawlish returned to the Jermyn Street flat. He paused at the foot of the stairs, and then said quietly: 'Are you sure Elvira has told you everything she knows?'

Robbie nodded.

'Yes. We're not holding anything back.'

Strains of radio music were coming from the lounge when he opened the door. Felicity leapt up quickly.

'Are the others all right?'

'All of us are,' said Dawlish promptly. He caught a glimpse of his reflection in a mirror and grinned. 'I need a wash and change.' He made for the bathroom door. 'Then I'll go and see Whitewash, and find out what he thinks about it.'

Felicity followed him. She looked troubled.

He kissed her. 'Cheer up, sweetheart. Tell me what you make of Elvira.'

Felicity hesitated.

'I think she's all right, but she's very worried about her uncle.'

'Is she engaged to Robbie?'

'No-o,' said Felicity.

'H'm,' said Dawlish. 'So they're not engaged. Did you get any idea why?'

'Reading between the lines, I'd say it was the uncle. He's pretty well dependent on Elvira just now. She feels she should be looking after him, and I think that makes her hesitate to say "yes" to Robbie.'

'Judging from what I've seen of the old boy I should say he was perfectly capable of exacting such a sacrifice. A strong personality, and Elvira's completely under his thumb.' Dawlish finished drying his hands and dived for the bedroom. 'Still, we don't have to worry about that at the moment, Robbie must work out his own future.'

'And now supposing we talk about something else,' suggested Felicity. 'What are you going to do now?'

'See Whitewash,' answered Dawlish promptly.

'And after that?'

'Well, we'll have to wait to see what turns up.'

Felicity eyed him straightly for a moment.

'You've got something else in mind, Pat. What is it?'

'That isn't entirely true,' said Dawlish slowly. 'But I do expect a most unholy crack before long. Kohn—if he *is* Kohn—tried hard to get me converted to the jewel theory, but the affair at Hampstead is an admission that he's failed.'

'Pat,' Felicity spoke quietly, 'you've been as near to death this time as ever you've been. They could have killed you.'

Dawlish smiled.

'We don't have to take the will for the deed! Kohn made a mistake, and we're benefiting from it.' He took up collar and tie, put them on, and then looked for his tunic. Felicity helped him into it, and when he had buttoned it he put an arm about her shoulders. 'I don't think it's going to be long, darling. There's one thing Kohn hasn't tried yet, and that is to work through you. Please God he won't. Can you stick it here, without going out, for another twenty-four hours?'

Felicity forced a smile.

'Yes, of course Pat.'

A few moments later they joined the others. Robbie had just finished a brief account of what had happened. Tim Jeremy looked at Dawlish with a mock scowl.

'I resent being left out of it,' he said firmly.

'You'll be in it before we've finished,' Dawlish assured him. 'At the moment there isn't much to do.'

Beresford rubbed his chin.

'That's true, Pat. D'you know, if Kohn hadn't shown himself you wouldn't know that he existed.'

Dawlish grinned. 'I've realised that, yes. But obviously we have him worried, otherwise he would have stayed out of the way. Still, I'd like to know why he thought it necessary to turn up at Westbourne.'

'Isn't it obvious?' asked Elvira. 'Surely he knew that you had been working on Hennessy, and wanted to stop you. Robbie says that Rosstein talked about Hennessy.'

'That's so,' admitted Dawlish. 'But I didn't believe all that Rosstein said by a long way. Whether we started the ball rolling by going to Dorchester or Wimborne we don't know yet. Well now, work for us all! Ted, you'll come with me, in case I'm followed. Tim, will you take Robbie and the girls out to an early dinner? They'll be glad of a change from the gloom of the flat. I suggest Oddenini's as being the nearest.' He glanced at his watch. 'It's half past six. Can you be back by eight?'

'What about me?' demanded Tony.

'Someone ought to stay here and pick up messages,' said Dawlish. 'Do you mind?'

'Drat you,' said Tony. 'Yes, I do.'

He stayed, nevertheless.

Dawlish and Ted went towards Audeley Street a few minutes afterwards. Two of Trivett's men were in Jermyn Street, but no one else was loitering there. They went a long way round, but neither of them saw any signs that they were followed.

Ted strolled towards the far end of the street, while Dawlish was admitted to the Colonel's house, and taken straight up to the study. Whitehead was alone. He waved a hand to a chair beside the fireplace.

'So you're still making things happen?'

'They're still happening, anyhow,' returned Dawlish. 'Have you any further news?'

'Not a great deal. As you suggested, I've had our fellows and the police tracing the man Kohn, and his relatives. There were two brothers Kohn, English born of naturalised English parents; the father a German, the mother an Austrian. They settled here some time before the last war. The sons had a good education. The elder, Marius Kohn, was last heard of in China. He hasn't been known to be in this country for ten years, but, as you know, he had a police record. The younger, Saul, lived in Bayswater, and was a commission agent for an insurance company, and did other odds and ends of business. Marine insurance among them. He wasn't suspected of any law-breaking until the rationing, when he went into the black market. There's an interesting corrollary to that, Dawlish.'

Dawlish said evenly:

'According to Bateson he committed suicide after he was arrested. It could have been murder.'

Whitehead's heavy lids were raised abruptly.

'My oath, Dawlish, you do get there! Yes, it could have been murder. He was poisoned after eating some sweets. It was believed he managed to take the poison himself, but the sweets were brought in while he was under remand by a business friend. We can't trace the friend, but—' Whitehead shrugged. 'It could easily be that his employers were afraid that he would talk.'

'Pretty ruthless chap if the other Kohn is our man,' said Dawlish. 'Anything else?'

Whitehead shrugged. 'I've had several urgent telephone calls from Downing Street demanding action. There's a strong suggestion that everyone we suspect should be detained. Do you think we've reached the time when we should do that?'

'I do not!' exclaimed Dawlish energetically. 'We haven't any trace of these people except through the names and addresses on hand. Now that Rosstein's dead and Hennessy's missing, we've the men Train and Cornwallis, and Mrs. Benn, to deal with. They need to be watched closely. Their detention wouldn't help us at all.'

'Ye-es,' admitted Whitehead. 'I rather agree with you, but I doubt if we'll be able to stall much longer. The murder of Rosstein has worried both the Home Office and the India Office. However, I think you're all right for another twelve hours. What do you propose to do?'

'Nothing, until we've some news of Hennessy. Or—' Dawlish smiled—'things start happening to us.'

Whitehead frowned.

'Supposing we don't hear of Hennessy, and nothing starts happening?'

'It will,' said Dawlish with assurance. 'Kohn is much too worried to let things stay as they are. From the first I've let him and his men believe that I know more than I do. It's an obvious policy, and it will get results.'

'So operations are suspended,' murmured Whitehead.

'As far as I'm concerned, they've got to be,' said Dawlish, 'but you needn't let that worry you, sir, Kohn will act before long, and if he doesn't I'll put myself in a position where action is invited.' He seemed amused. 'Now I've something to report—'

He talked for a quarter of an hour about Elvira's statements. Whitehead nodded from time to time, making no comment until Dawlish had finished. Then:

'So we know why Rennett was on the list but not on the board of the oil company. That's an advance of a kind, anyhow. We know why Bateson wanted to kill Graham, too, but the man Kohn is obviously more important than Hennessy. He tried to kill him as he tried to kill Rosstein, of course. What I can't see is why he let them live if they were so dangerous to him.'

Dawlish said: 'That's understandable enough. He wanted them to work for him. They have been working for him. How and when I don't know, but we can take it for granted that they were useful members of his organisation. But you've made one error I think.'

'About what?'

'The attempt to kill Hennessy.'

'Well, wasn't one made?' demanded Whitehead.

'Not by a long way, sir. Hennessy—'

'Damn it, he was within an ace of being blown up!'

'He was no nearer being blown up than you are at this moment,' said Dawlish with assurance. 'It's true it looked that way, as it was meant to do. But nobody can disappear so completely without help. Moreover we've since discovered that these people didn't use a time bomb at Hampstead. What would be a better cover for Hennessy than the set-up at The Lees and his "narrow escape"?'

'I don't quite follow you,' admitted Whitehead.

'I mean that Hennessy knew that the place was mined, but almost certainly operated the switch which caused the explosion himself,' said Dawlish.

Whitehead frowned.

'It's possible, I suppose. But why should he disappear if he wanted to look like a victim?'

'Because he had orders from Kohn to disappear. Kohn's our King Pin,' went on Dawlish, 'or rather, he's the operative leader, with someone else behind him. I think I know who,' he added slowly.

'Do you, by George! Who is it?'

'I'll make sure before I name anyone,' said Dawlish. 'It's a complicated set-up, sir, and I may be wrong. I think Hennessy has been organising this thing in England, that Kohn has been sent to make sure that he doesn't run off the rails, and that our unknown is the main organiser, who usually works abroad. I think too,' went on Dawlish, 'that he's no more and no less than the Far East fifth columnist Number 1, who worked well in the Straits Settlements and in Burma, but had to come here to get preparations ready for really big-scale work in India. Once here, he discovered trouble—I think Hennessy was probably trying to double-cross him, and that forced him to stay here for a bit. But for that we wouldn't be as advanced as we are.'

Whitehead's expression was troubled.

'So you think we're advanced, do you? I think you've made it a damned sight more confused than it was.'

Dawlish smiled one-sidedly.

'I hope you'll change your mind before the next twenty-four hours are passed, sir. Is there anything else?'

'If you won't talk I can't make you,' growled Whitehead. 'Where are you going now?'

'To see Trivett,' said Dawlish promptly.

Ted was waiting in the street, and had nothing to report. They took a taxi to Scotland Yard, and were not followed.

They found Trivett in the canteen, and joined him in an early supper.

'Any news?' asked Dawlish.

'Yes and no. The man who was injured at The Lees died.'

'Oh,' said Dawlish blankly. 'Poor devil. Have you traced him?'

'No. There was nothing on him to identify him.' Trivett paused. 'Has Miss Templeton any idea who he was?'

Dawlish stared. 'Elvira, of course!'

'If she knew him she would have said so,' put in Beresford.

'Ye-es.' Dawlish seemed doubtful. 'I shouldn't have forgotten to ask, all the same.'

Trivett bit into a sandwhich, and then mumbled: 'What are you going to do next, Pat?'

'Play the waiting game. As I told Whitehead, Kohn is bound to try something. Whether it will be another crack at me or not, I don't know. But I'll tell you what I expect.'

'That's nice of you,' said Trivett sardonically.

'Yes, I think so too.' Dawlish lowered his voice, Ted and Trivett straining forward to catch every word. 'I think that Kohn will reason that before long I'll go to the other three addresses. I think he'll forestall me, and that you'll soon be having word that all three people have left their houses. I think that your men will be able to follow them, and that they'll all be traced to the same place. Kohn will take it for granted that I will go to try to see them.'

'Well?' asked Ted.

'I shall,' said Dawlish amiably.

'And what kind of obituary would you like?' demanded Trivett. 'Thus died Dawlish, who knew what to expect and got it?'

Dawlish grinned. 'Granted that I may be wrong, I expect something on the lines I've mentioned, and if it comes I think you ought to have a squad or two of men ready, Bill. Say, for instance, they go to Rennett's house—'

'Is there any reason why they should?' asked Trivett swiftly.

'Well, he's not there, and it's a quiet spot near the sea and well-placed for dark doings,' said Dawlish. 'But wherever it is, I'll go down with Ted and the others, leaving the girls at the flat and relying on your people to make sure nothing happens to them. I'll take my party in, and yours will watch for events,' he added.

'It's all too vague,' declared Trivett.

'Heaven help us, you don't expect a signed confession, do you?' cried Dawlish.

A voice could be heard calling: 'Telephone for Superintendent Trivett!'

Dawlish and Beresford watched the Superintendent as he strode across the room.

'How much are you pulling his leg, Pat?' Ted asked.

'I'm not,' Dawlish assured his friend.

He was looking towards Trivett, who was slowly returning. On the Superintendent's handsome face there was an expression which drove the smiles from Dawlish's eyes.

A silence had fallen over the canteen as Trivett drew up with them. He said gravely:

'It's not good, Pat. Felicity and the Templeton girl were snatched outside Oddenini's. Graham was, too. Tim Jeremy is badly hurt, and so are the two of my men who were following.'

CHAPTER TWENTY-ONE

THE ROAD TO WHERE?

Dawlish's eyes were blank and expressionless.

Then he said:

'The obvious thing, of course. They always do the obvious thing.' He paused. 'Did anyone manage to follow them?'

'No.'

'What happened?'

'Someone threw a tear-gas bomb. Tim realised what was happening and pulled his gun, but he was run down by a car. My men tried to board it, and were shot. When the confusion died away, the others were gone. There isn't even a record of the car number.'

'It wouldn't help if there was,' said Dawlish. 'It would be changed.' He looked at Ted bleakly. 'I was wrong, you see. I shouldn't have eased off, I should have kept them at the flat.' He spoke in a low-pitched, bitter voice. 'And we've no idea where they've gone.'

'Every address we've got is being watched,' Trivett assured him.

'And Kohn knows it,' said Dawlish. He paused, and then

added: 'My God, there's nothing we can do, d'you understand that? Nothing at all.' He turned to the door. 'We'd better get to the flat, Ted. Kohn will be calling or phoning. Draw your men off, Bill, will you?'

'From the flat?'

'Yes. Unless you can arrange for someone to watch from a house opposite. No one must be seen. Any approach to the watching point needs to be made from the back. The flat's been under observation by Kohn's men all the time, of course.'

Dawlish and Beresford left the Yard and walked to the Embankment. Neither man spoke for some time, then Dawlish said:

'If anything goes really wrong, Ted, there'll only be me to blame.'

'It'll work out,' Beresford muttered.

'Yes. One way or the other.'

They lapsed into silence, walking slowly towards St. James's Park.

Thirty-five minutes had passed before they reached the flat. There was no sign of Trivett's men, and no one appeared to be watching the house. Dawlish went up the stairs without speaking, put his key in the lock, and then paused.

'Someone might be in there,' Ted murmured.

'Ye-es,' said Dawlish. 'It isn't likely, though. Kohn wants me to make a journey, he wouldn't have gone to this trouble if he didn't. If it were just a case of killing me, the snatch wouldn't have been necessary.'

Nevertheless he pushed the door open and stepped swiftly to one side. There was no sound, and after a pause Dawlish drew his revolver and went in. No one was in the little hall, but from the lounge Tony Grayling called:

'Is that you, Pat?'

'Yes,' said Dawlish.

The tone of his voice brought Grayling to the door in a hurry. Dawlish nodded and stepped past him, then went into his room. Tony looked at Ted, who shrugged his shoulders and then explained quietly.

The ringing of the telephone startled them, for the tension in the flat was great. Dawlish returned quickly, snatching up the receiver. 'Yes, speaking.' He moved a hand to Ted, who slipped into the kitchen, where there was another telephone, on a separate line. He dialled 999 and asked for the call to be traced, mentioning Trivett's name, and Dawlish's.

Meanwhile Dawlish heard Kohn's hollow voice say:

'You have doubtless heard what has happened, Dawlish.'

'Yes,' said Dawlish.

'Had you been wise, you could have prevented it,' said Kohn softly.

'My dear Kohn,' said Dawlish, with an effort which did not show in his voice: 'Do you seriously think I didn't *expect* that to happen?'

Kohn snapped: 'You didn't stop it!'

Dawlish knew that he had his man puzzled. He was trying desperately to make some capital out of a virtual disaster. His friends, watching him, could judge the struggle within him, and were amazed at the quiet confidence in his voice, the apparent casualness of his manner.

'Just why?' asked Kohn.

'As I told Graham earlier,' said Dawlish, 'there are times when personal issues have to be side-stepped. This is a national one. I had to take chances, Kohn, and I've taken them. But you've made your final blunder.'

There was a pause. He heard a sound at the other end of the wire, as if Kohn took in a sharp breath.

'I'm not bluffed that way, Dawlish, and I didn't call you for a talk. You'll do as you're told if you want the women to be unharmed.'

'Listen to me,' Dawlish said harshly. 'From time immemorial people like you have tried tricks of this kind. The idea's always the same, to put up a secondary issue and by it draw attention away from the main one. You've got Miss Deverall and the others, but they remain a secondary issue. Whatever happens to them won't make an iota of difference to you, except—' He stopped for a moment, and then went on: 'Except that if they're hurt I'll deal with you myself, and not leave you to the authorities.'

Kohn said sharply: 'You'll never lay your hands on me!'

'If I wanted I could come and get you now,' said Dawlish.

There was another sharp intake of breath at the other end of the wire. In the flat Tony and Ted watched Dawlish in startled silence, wondering what was in his mind and yet realising that his chief purpose was to make Kohn feel uncertain about this, his latest move.

'You don't know what you're saying,' Kohn said at last.

'You poor fool,' said Dawlish. 'You poor, deluded fool. I could have had you under arrest within an hour of the start of this business, *but I didn't want you*. I want your leader, and I'm going to get him. Is that clear enough?'

'Dawlish,' said Kohn unsteadily, 'you're talking for the sake of it. Listen to me. Make the police withdraw from Rennett's house, and you yourself go down there. I will meet you at the house. If there are any policemen with you, I shall kill your friends.'

'The same cheap clap-trap,' Dawlish said. 'You won't get away with it, Kohn. I'm not coming.'

'You'll regret it if you don't.'

'All right, I'll regret it.'

There was no reply, but the line went dead.

Dawlish turned and regarded his friends.

'Well, Kohn doesn't know what to make of it,' he said. 'And I'm damned if I do!'

The telephone in the other room rang sharply, and he stepped through. A Yard man told him that the call had been traced to a telephone kiosk in Kingston-on-Thames, and that Captain Dawlish could rest assured that if the caller could be found it would be done.

Dawlish replaced the receiver and told the others. 'They won't get there in time, of course, he'll make sure of that. Oh damn the phone!'

It rang again, insistently. He lifted the receiver and heard Trivett's voice. He listened for some seconds, still watched by the others, who looked as helpless as they felt. Dawlish said 'yes' and 'no', then promised to ring Trivett back.

'What was that?' asked Ted.

'Bill. The first guess was on the mark. Mrs. Benn has left her house, Train has gone from Fulham, and Cornwallis from Little Granley. They're all being followed. If I only knew what to do!' he exclaimed. 'If I could be sure what course was the best, if—' He stopped abruptly.

'According to Kohn, Felicity's at Westbourne,' said Tony. 'Oughtn't we to go down there?'

'That's what Kohn wants,' said Dawlish harshly. 'To keep us out of the way while he gets on with his big show! What's he going to do? What—'

He stopped abruptly, but this time there was a light in his eyes.

'The obvious thing!' he snapped at last. 'Now we're at this stage there's no safety for any of them in the country, they've got to get out. Where will they go from?' He paced across the room, turned and paced back. 'Trivett might get word from one of his men, we'll have to wait on that. Meanwhile—' He drew a deep breath. 'We'll go to Westbourne after all.'

'But—' began Tony.

'We'll let Kohn think I've fallen for it,' continued Dawlish. 'We'll go in a police car fitted with the radio, and Trivett can have a message sent to us. Right?' He did not wait for an answer but stepped to the telephone and called Trivett. It took only a few minutes to make the arrangements. Trivett promised to have a car ready for them within twenty minutes.

By then it was growing dusk.

The police car was waiting for them outside the Yard, and once there Dawlish joined Trivett, who was at the wheel himself, while Ted and Tony followed in the Lagonda.

In the back of the police car were two Yard men, with a radio receiving and transmitting set. They were on the other side of Staines when the first call came from Scotland Yard.

Headquarters calling Superintendent Trivett. Headquarters calling Superintendent Trivett. Man followed from Fulham, arrived The Lees, Wimborne, Dorset. No action taken, no action taken. Headquarters calling . . .

Trivett looked in the darkness towards Dawlish.

'To Hennessy's place.'

'It looks like it,' said Dawlish. 'I take it that none of your people were hurt?'

'If that had been so we would have heard,' Trivett assured him. 'I gave instructions for details of any attack or attempted attack to be transmitted.'

'Good man,' said Dawlish.

Once past Sunningdale, Trivett took the Basingstoke-Winchester road, and they were a few miles from the cathedral town when the second message came through. It was exactly the same as the first except that instead of 'man followed from Fulham' it was 'woman followed from Ewell'.

'So the simple-minded housekeeper is there too,' said Dawlish. 'We're getting on.'

'Are you going straight to Westbourne?' asked Trivett. 'We'll get to Wimborne quicker if we go the other way.'

'Leave it a bit, will you?' said Dawlish.

The third call, concerning Cornwallis of Little Granley, was received when they reached Romsey. Again Trivett asked whether Dawlish wanted to go to Westbourne, or thought it wiser to go to The Lees.

'Westbourne, I think,' said Dawlish. 'I can't get rid of the feeling that we're being followed or watched. I can't be in two places at once, and I want Kohn to think I've fallen for the bait after all. I can't think beyond that,' he added, and Trivett glanced at him curiously, thinking that he had never known Dawlish quite so uncertain of himself.

'Well, The Lees house is covered,' said Trivett. 'The Dorset people are there in strength, and on learning this my people will ask them to redouble their efforts. I don't see how any of the three can get away.'

'No, that's just it,' said Dawlish. 'I can't, either. They haven't given much trouble, and your fellows have found it easy to follow them. There's been no attack. Why hasn't there?'

'Kohn can't do everything,' protested Trivett.

'He's done everything he wants to, so far.' They ran into Lyndhurst, then continued through the New Forest, past the spot where Dawlish had been found unconscious. The moon was not yet up, but behind them there was a glow as it rose in the sky. Once Trivett braked sharply when the shape of a pony loomed up in the road.

They were in Christchurch when Dawlish said:

'Pull up, Bill, will you?'

Trivett drew into the side of the road. Tony and Ted pulled up immediately behind the police car, and the two men hurried forward, meeting Dawlish on the pavement. He told them what had happened, and Tony asked:

'Then what are we waiting for?'

'For an idea to break,' said Trivett gruffly. 'Pat, one of these days you won't get an idea just when you want it.' The policeman spoke feelingly, and Dawlish eyed him in the faint light of the moon. He could sympathise with Trivett, who had general orders to follow his instructions but who was doubtless thinking that both The Grove and The Lees should be raided simultaneously. True, both places were watched by the police, but there would be no raid until Dawlish gave the word.

Dawlish was afraid to give it.

He was so desperately anxious not to go wrong. The whole crazy affair had happened so quickly, there had been no time for concentrated thinking.

Dawlish was trying to pierce a blanket of depression. The idea Trivett talked of was needed, but it must be one that was the result of a logical train of thought. There must be an explanation of Kohn's kidnapping of the trio, of his telephone talk. It could be the obvious thing, for it was obvious enough for Kohn to expect him to visit Westbourne.

'We're losing time,' Trivett said impatiently.

'Ye-es,' said Dawlish, and there was a new note in his voice, a lighter feeling within him. 'Yes, Bill, we're losing time. What did I tell Kohn? That I wouldn't fall for the obvious. What did he do? Almost beg me to come to Westbourne, and then arrange for the others to leave and to be followed to a place where we can find them. Bill, isn't it likely that Kohn would know that I would choose to *avoid doing what he asked?* Isn't he going to reason that I'll do anything but that?'

'It could be,' Trivett admitted slowly.

Dawlish snapped: 'It is! There's a telephone over the road, I saw the kiosk. Phone the Bournemouth police, Bill. Ask them to get Medway and his men moving at The Lees to keep watch on the people there. Tell them to go in strength, but do nothing unless the visitors try to escape. And then—and then,' he added, 'ask them to take their own people, the Bournemouth men, away from The Grove. Before you do, have your men here radio word to the Yard that we're going to Wimborne right away.'

'What the devil *are* you going to do?' demanded Trivett.

'Go to Westbourne, when the police are away and when Kohn thinks we're hot-foot to Wimborne. We weren't followed, but I couldn't believe that there wasn't some check on what we were doing. A radio check, of course, they're listening in! Get that message sent back, Bill, and Bournemouth called.'

Trivett gave rapid instructions to his men, and then hurried across to the telephone. Ted and Tony regarded Dawlish, the latter with increasing exasperation.

'I suppose you do know what you're doing,' he said.

'Yes,' said Dawlish crisply. 'The thing Kohn doesn't expect me to do.'

'But—'

'Hold it, Tony,' Ted said easily. 'Pat's probably right. Kohn would take it for granted that he'd do what he thought was the thing that mattered, worry about the bigger game not the personal one. Right, Pat?'

Dawlish nodded.

'The stronger the bait the more likely Pat would be to resist it,' added Beresford.

'But why the devil did Kohn talk of Rennett's house if he doesn't want Pat to go there?' demanded Tony.

'That's why,' said Dawlish positively. 'A bluff and now we'll double it.' He turned. 'All right Bill?'

'Yes,' said Trivett. 'They're moving their men away from Rennett's place immediately, and they've contacted Medway at Wimborne. Now what are we going to do?'

'Go to Rennett's place,' said Dawlish, 'and take our time.'

In a house not far from 18, The Grove, Kohn and Hennessy sat talking. Opposite them was Catten, crouching in front of a receiving set. There was absolute silence in the room. Hennessy was staring tensely at Catten, Kohn was leaning back, rigid but less on edge than Hennessy. They sat like that for a long time, and then Catten raised a hand.

The others leaned forward.

A few seconds more passed in silence, and then Catten turned, his eyes glistening.

'It's okay, it's okay! They're going to Wimborne!' He snatched the earphones off and added loudly: 'Boss, I hand it to you, they're going to Wimborne'

'Thank God for that!' exclaimed Hennessy. 'We can move now, Kohn.'

'Not at once,' said Kohn tonelessly. 'Catten, go out and watch the other house. Report any movements of the police immediately. If they are there after another fifteen minutes, deal with them as you have dealt with others.'

'Okay,' said Catten.

He went out, and while he was away Hennessy and Kohn sat motionless, saying nothing, until Hennessy muttered:

'What time did Rennett get back to his house?'

'Two hours ago.'

'Can we do it all right when he's there?'

'Yes,' said Kohn.

Hennessy shrugged his shoulders, then stood up and paced the room restlessly.

His footsteps echoed about the house, and were heard by Felicity, Elvira, and Robbie, in the room above. All three of them were bound hand and foot, and gagged.

The pacing footsteps stopped.

They heard a door bang downstairs, and then a high-pitched voice followed by muttering. They did not know that Catten had entered hurriedly, his little eyes glistening with satisfaction.

'The dicks are moving, Boss, they're on the way.'

'Talk less loudly,' rebuked Kohn. 'Are all of them going?'

'Sure, I've seen them get into a car, five of them. That's all there were, Boss, we're all set.'

'What are we going to do with the people upstairs?' Hennessy asked abruptly.

'We shall leave them where they are until their use in influencing Dawlish is over. Then of course we shall dispose of them.' Kohn smiled, thin-lipped. 'All of them have seen you. Hennessy, and could give evidence against you. We must make sure that you can face the world again, a much-maligned man but one who has been gravely misunderstood. Don't we?'

'Come on, let's get to Rennett's house,' said Hennessy sharply. 'I'm tired of waiting.'

CHAPTER TWENTY-TWO

VISITORS TO THE GROVE

James Rennett sat propped against his pillows, his pipe drooping from his lips. Standing at the foot of the bed was the nurse who had come with him from the nursing home. She liked him no more now than she had when he had first roared an order to her, and she said spitefully:

'It would serve you right if you were left on your own.'

'Then get out with you, you besom!' roared Rennett. 'Off with you, and leave me alone. Fidgeting here, poking your nose there, have done with it!'

'If it weren't for my duty—' began the nurse.

She moved stiffly to the door, then suddenly stopped in her tracks. The first shrill note of a scream died to a gurgle as a hand closed over her mouth. She slumped to the floor.

Rennett stared at the door as Kohn stepped through, followed by Hennessy.

The sailor did not move, even when Catten entered and leered across at him. The silence of the movements of the others was uncanny, but Rennett's silence was the most unnatural thing of all. He watched while Kohn approached one side of the bed and Hennessy the other. Then:

'What do you want?' rasped Rennett.

Hennessy leaned forward, peering into the sick man's red-rimmed eyes.

'First of all, you,' he said. 'And then those jewels, Rennett. I'm not fooling now. Where are they?'

Rennett spat at him: 'Find out!'

'I'm going to,' said Hennessy softly, 'and while I'm finding them I'm going to make you suffer. I'll teach you to set your spies on me, I'll make you pay for your damned insults.' He drew his hand back, and would have struck the sailor had Kohn not interposed.

'That will do, Hennessy.'

Rennett grunted. 'I'm glad to see one of you has some sense. Send that grinning cheetah away from my bed!' he snapped, glaring at Catten.

Catten opened his lips, but Kohn said swiftly:

'Catten, go downstairs and keep watch. You should not be here.'

'Okay, okay,' muttered Catten sullenly.

He turned and left the room, while Hennessy stared at Kohn, obviously not pleased that he had been interrupted.

'Do you want the stuff or don't you?' he asked petulantly.

'All in good time, Hennessy, there are many other things to discuss. Among them—'

Kohn paused, the pulled up a chair and sat down. Rennett sat eyeing them watchfully but saying nothing while Kohn talked, and after a while Hennessy's mouth dropped open in astonishment.

Of the four men in the two cars, only Dawlish seemed fully satisfied that they were doing the right thing. Nearing The Grove,

Trivett slowed down, and soon the four men were standing together on the pavement.

'Two on each side, I think,' said Dawlish. 'Coming with me, Bill?'

'Yes,' said Trivett shortly.

They stopped by the gates of Number 18.

'This is where Elvira slipped,' Dawlish said. 'It was quite a night, Bill, you should have been here.' He turned into the drive, and as he did so caught a glimpse of a man moving in the porch of the house.

It was Catten.

In the shrubbery another man was waiting, and at the back 'Polly' was on guard. 'Polly' heard the movement in the grounds and hurried round to investigate. Trivett, who had an automatic in his hand, saw the man coming and stepped towards him, saying simply:

'Stay where you are.'

It was so great a surprise that 'Polly' stopped. But only for a second. As he moved for his gun, Trivett jumped forward, striking at the man's arm. An automatic clattered to the ground. Trivett struck at 'Polly' with his free hand, and sent the man reeling against the wall.

By then Beresford and Grayling were in the drive.

Near them, rigid in alarm, was the third guard. He drew a gun and raised it carefully, but before he could fire, Tony Grayling poked an automatic into his back.

Inside the house there was a clatter of footsteps and a shout. Beresford reached Tony and his captive, and using his revolver as a club struck the guard on the temple. The man fell with hardly a sound.

Grayling grunted:

'Well, that was easy.'

'Yes. Trivett's got someone, too.'

'Why, it's the Pollittzer bird, without his feathers!'

Beresford grinned at Trivett, and then with a swift movement clubbed 'Polly'. He did not wait to hear Trivett's disapproval, but swung round to the house, adding: 'Pat'll need us.'

Dawlish was half-way up the stairs of the house by then.

Catten was ahead of him, and had rushed into Rennett's bedroom.

Dawlish heard the man gasping out his news.

He stepped across the landing and pressed close against the wall. The bedroom door opened and the snout of an automatic poked through. Three shots spat from it, the roar echoing about the house. Tersely Dawlish called down the stairs:

'The front bedroom window is to the right of the porch. Watch it, Ted!'

Beresford snapped to Grayling:

'Come on,' and the two men hurried back into the drive, while Trivett hesitated, then made a dash up the stairs, defying the bullets. He reached the wall beside Dawlish.

'How many are there, do you know?'

'No, but we've caught them on the hop,' said Dawlish with satisfaction. 'Stay here, Bill.'

Bent double he crept past the doorway. His movement was noticed, and a shot whizzed over his head. There was a bleak smile on his face as he watched the door from the other side and then raised his voice:

'Kohn, you're caught, you can't make it.'

There was no reply, and Trivett whispered something which Dawlish did not catch. Dawlish shook his head, and called again.

'All right, Kohn, I'm coming, and I'm starting with a hand-grenade.'

At last Kohn spoke, his voice a little unsteady.

'Dawlish, understand that Rennett is in here, and any injury to me will be injury to him.'

'That's too bad,' said Dawlish. 'Tell him to duck under the bedclothes. As for you, you've two minutes to come out, and if you're still in there at the end of them I'm throwing my egg.'

As he spoke, he kicked the door open.

He saw Catten a couple of yards inside the room with a gun in his hand. Both of them fired simultaneously. Dawlish felt a bullet go through his coat, as Catten fell backwards.

Behind the man, on the other side of the bed, were Kohn and Hennessy. There was a brief, but spirited, shooting match. Then, from the door Trivett said quietly:

'Stay there, Kohn.'

Kohn, on his way to the window, stopped quite still. Dawlish straightened up, seeing Hennessy on the floor and Rennett staring at him and Trivett.

Then Rennett roared:

'My oath, Dawlish, you've got them!' Kohn stood absolutely still, his pallid face motionless, his eyes in shadows. He kept his gun pointing towards the floor.

Dawlish said: 'Pop down and tell the others it's all right here, Bill, will you, but there might be new arrivals; nothing about Kohn will surprise me.' When Trivett had gone Dawlish said steadily:

'Kohn, where are the others?'

There was a note of triumph in Kohn's answer.

'They are the only cards I have left, Dawlish. My freedom will be set against theirs.'

'So,' said Dawlish. 'Haven't I made it clear that I'm not mixing the two issues?' He stood easily with a gun in either hand, but had an eye on Hennessy as well as the pale-faced man. 'I did give you an alternative, Kohn. I said that if anything happened to them I would handle you myself.'

Kohn said: 'You cannot. You have a policeman with you.'

Dawlish smiled a little grimly.

'Well, well, our Kohn appeals to the police! I shouldn't rely too much on *that,* for what the eye doesn't see . . . Now, where are they?'

'I shall not tell you,' said Kohn stubbornly.

Dawlish shrugged.

'Please yourself,' he said. 'Hennessy, perhaps you will start talking.'

He was just too late to stop the shooting.

He had been watching Kohn's gun, but had sent a single glance towards Hennessy, and in that split second Kohn had fired.

In front of Dawlish's eyes a hole appeared in Hennessy's forehead. The man had reared upwards with a last desperate cry, then sagged downwards, hitting the floor.

Trivett came hurrying in.

'What was that? I heard—'

He stopped, for he saw Hennessy lying face upwards. Rennett stared tense-eyed at Dawlish. Kohn did not move. He needed watching, although he must have known that if he fired at Dawlish or Trivett he would be shot in turn. It was possible, however, that the man would go to any lengths to add to the damage he had already caused.

'Bill,' said Dawlish very slowly, 'it is true, is it not, that you received a Home Office order, asking you to give Colonel Whitehead and his nominees—of whom I am one—all the help they required, and to act under their direction?'

'Yes,' said Trivett.

'Did you hear that?' Dawlish demanded of Kohn.

The man said nothing, but the tip of his tongue came out and ran along his lips.

'I think that Miss Templeton, Felicity, and Robbie Graham

are about somewhere,' continued Dawlish. 'If you will take the three prisoners downstairs, and with Beresford and Grayling find out what you can from them, I will talk to Kohn on his own.'

'I see,' said Trivett tonelessly. 'What about Rennett?'

'I don't think he'll be in the way,' said Dawlish. 'He's probably as anxious to find Elvira as I am to find Felicity. Another thing, Bill. There's a telephone downstairs. Will you get as many of the local police as can be spared to come here and join in the search, and prepare them against mines like those at Hampstead?'

Dawlish kept Kohn covered, and did not speak until the door closed behind Trivett. There was no sound in the room until Dawlish's voice came quietly, almost casually.

'You see, Kohn, I have a *carte blanche* on this affair. There are things the police can't do, but as far as this business is concerned the only thing that matters is results. I'm going to get those results. Drop your gun.'

Kohn retained but did not move it.

'Drop your gun,' said Dawlish softly.

The man made no move. Dawlish fired. The bullet smacked against Kohn's gun, and smashed a finger. The gun dropped.

Rennett emitted a long, low-pitched whistle.

Dawlish said evenly: 'I'm not leaving this room until I have the full truth.'

'I am the only man who can release your fiancée,' said Kohn. 'She is with the others. They are in a house which will be destroyed in a little more than an hour. Do you understand that? It is her safety against mine, Dawlish.'

Dawlish's eyes and his voice were hard. 'You haven't any chance at all of getting away, Kohn, and I'm making no bargain with you.'

The brief silence which followed was tense, the suspense in

the atmosphere almost unbearable. None of the trio moved. Dawlish was hardly conscious of time. He did not know whether he could make Kohn talk, but believed that he had a fair chance of finding both the whole truth and the whereabouts of the prisoners. Kohn's attitude was unreal and unnatural, like the man himself; but he must be feeling the strain already, and the suspense while waiting would affect him further.

Dawlish said quietly:

'There are a lot of things you haven't realised from the beginning, Kohn. You didn't know what I knew, or what I put together. I'll tell you some of them. Hennessy, as a representative of Lex Oils, travelled in the Far East and made contact with Japanese and German agents. Lex Oils has never been more than an unimportant little independent company, but its directors were paid by Germany and Japan.'

'My oath!' roared Rennett. 'The ruddy traitors!'

'Not all of them knew,' continued Dawlish. 'Hennessy did, and Rosstein. Kohn was the liaison officer between the company and the Axis. The other directors, knowing that the company was insolvent, nevertheless drew handsome fees. After a time they were needed to do espionage work of a comparatively mild kind. They were told that their money would cease if they refused. To make sure that they obeyed, Kohn employed a man, Bateson, to frighten them. Apparently he succeeded. He also tried to frighten you, Rennett, because you were so curious about Hennessy.'

He paused, and Kohn sneered.

'You can't undo the work they've done, Dawlish.'

'I can stop them doing more,' said Dawlish. 'That's the thing that counts now. Complications came from what appeared to be a private feud between Hennessy and Rennett,' he continued. 'It would have mattered little but for the recall of Graham, and the fact that he came down here. Graham had to be silenced. Bateson tried to do it, failed, and talked to me. From then on you, Kohn, started a campaign of bluff. You killed Pollittzer and tried to get information about me through his impersonator. You killed Mrs. Arthurson in the hope that I would follow her trail, or that of the others. The only men who mattered were Hennessy and Rosstein, and to try to make me think Hennessy was just one of the victims, your shabby little man—who hasn't shown up yet—put over the attempted shooting. It looked convincing at the time, but any doubts I had about Hennessy's importance faded when I heard of the destruction of his house, and the way it was done. When he disappeared, Kohn, you thought I would concentrate on the others, but thanks to Miss Templeton I learned of the Lex Oils complication, and I went to Rosstein. Your trick there was clever. It missed because you overdid the preparations. Rosstein was too obviously jittery, and in view of your other killings I was quite sure that you wouldn't want him alive. Your policy by then was clear enough, Kohn; to kill everyone who might have talked.'

There was a moment of silence before Rennett exclaimed:

'You've worked it out damned well, Dawlish.'

Kohn said: 'It will serve no purpose. You are right, Dawlish, up to a point. But you will not achieve your main object. We shall go on whether I live or die. It is ordained that we shall. For years I have been working for the Führer, and—'

Dawlish snapped:

'We won't have any Hitler *heiling* play-acting now. I haven't finished yet. You did what you wanted in the Straits Settlements and in Burma, your organisation has worked up feeling among the natives, is doing so among Indian minorities. I've no doubt that in England you've been in contact with Indian leaders and commercial men who have influence in India, and I've no doubt that you've been trying to find what we propose to do there. You and your leader saw the danger signs over here and came to make sure that Hennessy did not talk.'

'Your discoveries will make no difference,' sneered Kohn. 'The work will go on, Dawlish. The cause is greater than the man.'

'My own thoughts exactly,' agreed Dawlish. 'There's someone else working with you, of course. Hennessy learned of him, and you were afraid that he would talk, that's why you killed him. But you needn't have troubled, Kohn. I told my Chief that I knew the identity of the real leader of the organisation, and now I'm going to tell you his name.'

Kohn drew a sharp breath.

'That is a lie!'

'Oh, don't waste your breath,' said Dawlish sharply. 'I know him as well as I know you.' He stood up abruptly, his gun still covering Kohn. 'He's the only man who has had an opportunity for making regular contact with your Far Eastern agents, the only man who has spent most of his life in the Far East, the man who made the mistake of telling a half truth to someone else and thus starting this business. He—'

Dawlish stopped abruptly.

Rennett drew his hand from beneath the sheets, and in it there was a small automatic. But the shot that came from it was a split-second later than the bullet that came from Dawlish's gun.

'Thanks, Rennett,' said Dawlish off-handedly. 'I wasn't quite sure, but I am now.'

CHAPTER TWENTY-THREE

MUCH MORE TO LEARN

The echoes of the shooting faded.

Rennett's breathing was harsh and laboured, and for the first time Kohn seemed really affected by what had happened. His mouth dropped open, and he leaned against the wall for support. Dawlish looked from him to Rennett and back again, and there was a smile on the big man's face.

'So we reach the end of this part of the race,' he said. 'You were afraid Hennessy was double-crossing you, and since Rennett had to come back, and was torpedoed, there was a good chance of watching Hennessy through him and his niece. The story of the jewels was handy, and Rennett lied to his niece about being attacked on the cliff and nearly killed. She was glad to help him; but she wrote to Robbie Graham, and you didn't like the sound of that. When he came back you got busy, but he was a difficult man to kill.'

Dawlish turned to Rennett.

'Then Kohn had one of his bright ideas. He tried to make me think that the real leakage was elsewhere, and he told Bateson to talk of meeting Graham at Liverpool, if he were caught. He promised Bateson he would look after him if that happened. He did look after him.'

Kohn said in a low voice:

'What don't you know?'

'Oh, there's much to learn,' said Dawlish off-handedly. 'But there wasn't a leakage of information about ship movements, it was a clever scheme to get us looking in the wrong place. Not bad, Kohn, but like all Germans you were a little too thorough, you created too many complications.' He went on more evenly: 'Now you're both caught, and the only issue outstanding is that of Felicity and Elvira. Where are they, Rennett?'

Rennett snapped:

'Find out!'

'So you've no regard for your niece's life?'

'The little idiot started this,' snarled Rennett. 'If she hadn't blabbed to Graham it wouldn't have happened.'

'You underestimated the Intelligence Department,' said Dawlish. 'It had to come sooner or later.' Inwardly he felt a cold terror, for in these two men there was a hatred which it was hard to measure, a lust now for vengeance and death; and they cared not what happened to Felicity and Elvira.

Kohn said slowly, and with more composure:

'Dawlish, I have made you an offer. I will repeat it. Their safety against mine and Rennett's.'

'No,' said Dawlish.

There was another silence, and then from outside there came a call:

'Pat, are you there?'

Dawlish paused, ears strained and heart beating fast. It was Ted's voice, and there was a chance that the prisoners had been found. Then he raised his voice, and a few minutes later

Beresford entered the room. He stared at Rennett for a moment, astonished, and then said hurriedly:

'We haven't found a thing. None of the swine downstairs will talk. But I've seen the little shabby customer—remember him?'

'Where is he?'

'He came out of a house in the next street,' said Beresford.

'Do you know which house?'

'Not for certain,' said Beresford. 'It was one of three. Trivett and the police have made a cordon round them.'

Kohn said in a harsh voice:

'Dawlish, listen to me! They are in a house near here and I can blow the place up when I want to. I shall do this before the police can get inside if you don't let me go. Understand that? I can blow it up *from here.*'

'You damned fool!' roared Rennett. 'That's just what he wanted to know!'

Dawlish eyed Kohn without expression.

'So there's a switch here,' he said evenly.

Kohn backed a pace.

He was nearing Rennett. He stood there glaring at Dawlish. His voice, when it came, was high and breathless.

'My foot is covering it, Dawlish. Get out of this room. Get out, or I'll blow their house up!'

'You are lying,' said Dawlish lightly. 'It isn't under your foot. And you needn't try to give force to his arguments, Rennett. Nothing in this world will persuade me to let either of you go. Ted, get Trivett to raid all three houses. I'm staying here.'

Beresford went out.

Dawlish looked at the two men without speaking. He was thinking of Felicity. She was not far from here, and in deadly danger. She had done nothing to deserve what was happening to her and it would not have happened but for him. He felt a wave of nausea, for a moment even wondered whether he could hold out. He did not know whether to believe that Kohn was treading on a switch which could send the other house up or not. His whole body cried out to be with the searchers as they approached the houses. But he trusted neither Kohn nor Rennett, believed they had a trick up their sleeves, and he dared not take the risk of going away. Whether the other house was blown up or not, he had to stay here.

He said: 'Rennett, how long have you been working for the Axis?'

'Longer than you'll ever know,' retorted Rennett. 'Kohn's told you the truth, it will go on whatever happens to us.'

'You're an Englishman,' said Dawlish wonderingly.

'Englishman be damned! I've put my money on the winner, and it stays there. I've had enough of wishy-washy politics, I'm a fascist and always have been. Damn the English, and damn all they stand for. You make me sick! You stand there like a fool and you can save your girl by opening your mouth, you can save her by letting Kohn and me go. You can't stop what's happening in India, you can't smash our organisation. You've broken it up in this country, but it'll be built again whether we do it or someone else. What kind of man are you? That girl's lying not a hundred yards from here, and in a few minutes she'll be blown sky-high. What do you do? You stand there and do nothing. *You can save her, Dawlish.* No one else can.'

Dawlish kept quite still.

The man's words hammered against his mind. He knew that there was truth in them, he knew that if he traded with these men there was a chance that he would find Felicity. The temptation was almost more than he could stand.

Kohn said:

'Dawlish, you can't be such a fool as to say no. Listen to me.

You've heard about the jewels, and they're not imaginary. I know where they are, and I can get them for you. A hundred thousand pounds-worth, enough to make you rich all your life. Your fiancée's life and a hundred thousand pounds!'

Dawlish thought:

Felicity, and a hundred thousand pounds. A house that might blow up.

Was Kohn treading on the switch?

If he shot Kohn, would it save the day?

He knew that it would not, fought against believing there was a chance that Kohn could control the explosion. This time it was almost certainly a time-bomb. It was the only safe way for them to work. On the other hand they had not expected his arrival. God, why wouldn't his mind clear? If only he could think coherently.

'Your girl's life,' said Rennett harshly.

'A hundred thousand pounds,' mouthed Kohn.

'Her life,' said Rennett softly. 'Understand that, Dawlish, her life, her *life*.'

'A fortune,' said Kohn, 'a fortune, Dawlish, yours for the asking.'

The words were hammering against Dawlish's brain. There must be a way of making these two men crack, there must be.

Then suddenly he moved.

The movement was so swift and unexpected that both the others backed away, Rennett on his pillows, Kohn against the wall.

Dawlish struck only twice, then stepped to the door, opened it, and called down:

'Police—come up, will you?'

Two men came hurrying, and he said swiftly:

'Handcuff the two men in there. Stay in the room until I come back, and don't go out on any pretext whatever. Is that clear?'

'Yes, sir,' said one of the men.

Dawlish nodded, and left them.

In the hall he met Sergeant Munk. Dawlish, with no time for finesse, said abruptly: 'Where are the others?'

Munk looked at him sharply: 'Turn right and right again.'

In the open air Dawlish felt better. The first turning to the right seemed an interminable distance. He saw it in the increasing moonlight, as well as a policeman who approached him sturdily, with every sign of being about to detain him.

'I'm sorry, sir, you can't pass here just now.'

'I'm Dawlish!' Dawlish said.

'Indeed, sir?' said the policeman politely. 'I'm sorry, but I've had orders to allow no one to pass until further notice.'

Dawlish drew a deep breath.

Precious seconds were ticking by, thoughts of Felicity were tormenting him. He was tempted to push past the man, even attack him, but it would only cause complications, and perhaps defeat. He took out his wallet and extracted the card which gave him full authority, The policeman was an unconscionable time examining it, but when he had finished he saluted smartly, and stood back.

'That's all right, sir.'

'Where are they?' demanded Dawlish.

'Third house along, first turning to the right.'

Dawlish broke into a run.

Although the night was cool his forehead and neck were running with perspiration, and he found breathing difficult. He reached the next corner at last, and, turning it, saw a number of people moving about the drive entrance to one of the houses. He raced towards them.

It was then that the explosion came.

The blast of it swept him from his feet, flinging him against a wall. The din of the eruption was in his ears, and the roar of licking flames.

It had happened, and he had been too late.

'God!' he thought. 'Felicity, oh my God!'

He reached his feet and staggered forward. In the moonlight the tottering building looked stark and grim. Men were moving amidst the wreckage in the garden. A man passed him at a run, and as he went forward fire leapt from the wrecked building.

Then he heard Beresford's voice, calling him.

CHAPTER TWENTY-FOUR

THE PUZZLE OF THE JEWELS IS SOLVED

'Pat!' called Beresford. 'Pat, are you all right?'

He came running, reaching Dawlish as the latter was nearing the drive gates. Dawlish had no idea of the sight he presented. He had suffered more from the blast than those nearer the building, and was hardly recognisable.

'Felicity?' he croaked.

Beresford gripped his forearm.

'Steady, Pat,' he said. 'She's all right, we got her out in time. And the others.'

Dawlish stared at him, and then slowly backed to the wall and leaned against it. A surge of relief passed over him, making him tremble. He stared into Beresford's anxious face, his lips parted, gulping great breaths of air.

'I thought—I thought—' He broke off.

People were flocking round them from nearby houses. The wardens already on the scene.

Trivett came from the wreckage to Dawlish and Beresford, leaving Tony Grayling with the other party.

'We were lucky, Pat.'

'Yes. One day I'll be able to thank you,' said Dawlish. 'But for the moment, Bill, we'd better get back to the other place. Kohn and Rennett were unconscious when I left them, but—'

'Rennett!' exclaimed Trivett.

Dawlish told him just enough to satisfy him before they reached 18 The Grove.

Hurrying up the stairs Dawlish pushed open the door in a sudden spasm of fear lest Kohn and Rennett had somehow contrived to get away. He could not believe that it was over, and they were helpless.

The two policemen had been busy. Kohn was lying by Rennett's side, the crooks handcuffed together. Both of them stared malignantly at Dawlish as the trio approached.

Dawlish began to talk to Trivett. He gave an outline of what he had already said to Rennett and Kohn, emphasising his reasons for suspecting the sailor.

Trivett listened with an air of profound relief—'Well, thank heavens—and you—that's over.'

'Not quite over,' said Dawlish quietly. 'Apart from the fact that we've got to find the Indian end of the organisation, there's the little matter of the jewels. Fifty-thousand pounds-worth, according to Rennett, a hundred thousand according to Kohn. I'm very curious about those jewels.'

'Why so?' asked Beresford.

'Because they don't fit in; they never have fitted in. Anyhow, we'll start looking around. Elvira's room would be a safe and logical place for them.'

But they were not in Elvira's room.

The police started to search the house thoroughly, testing floorboards, walls, and fireplaces. Before they had finished, Felicity and the others had been sent to a nearby hotel for the night, Kohn and Rennett were on the way to London under a strong guard, while the lesser members of the organisation were in the Bournemouth police cells.

Dawlish and Beresford flopped down on a bed in one of the spare rooms. They slept for several hours, and it was daylight when they awakened.

Trivett called them. Red-eyed and weary, he sank heavily on the foot of the bed.

'No luck,' he said lugubriously. 'I'm beginning to think that they've gone up in the explosion.'

'Not gems of that value,' said Dawlish. 'I can't believe it, Bill. I'm beginning to wonder whether they ever existed!' He laughed shortly. 'I've always thought there was something queer about those jewels.' He swung his legs from the bed, and eyed Trivett with a sympathetic scowl. 'You'd better take my place. You look all in.'

Trivett kicked off his shoes, and laid down.

Dawlish and Beresford washed, brushed their crumpled suits, and went in search of something to eat.

After a meal of sorts, Ted said:

'Are you going to the hotel, Pat?'

'I'd like to find those jewels,' persisted Dawlish. 'Of course, Kohn might have had them, not Rennett. The shabby little customer got away, too, there's no report of him. Find him, and we'll probably find the jewels.'

'I don't see why you're so anxious about them,' objected Beresford. 'They don't count against the rest, Pat.'

Dawlish, much brighter and with a buoyant feeling within him, regarded his friend with a look of exaggerated forbearance.

'Ted,' he said, 'listen to me. The papers from Singapore were stolen the same night as the jewels. Also, they were stolen by the same organisation. Now a jewel robbery would be sure to start the police working quickly, it would be an easier thing to start on than the papers, which few people knew about. Why did Hennessy and Rennett start that hare?'

'It's obvious,' declared Beresford. 'They wanted to distract attention from the main motive.'

'Ye-es, it could be.' Dawlish rubbed the side of his nose. 'Certainly it could be, Ted, but to me the risk seems greater than the chances warranted.'

'Are you trying to tell me that the jewels are tied up with the whole scheme?' demanded Beresford.

'I'm saying that it's possible that they are,' declared Dawlish. 'I—my God, Ted, what am I doing?' He pushed his chair back and stood up abruptly. 'The others, the people who went to The Lees! Come on!'

In ten minutes they were driving towards Wimborne. They had a Bournemouth sergeant with them, while word had been left for a message to be handed to Trivett as soon as he woke up.

There was little traffic, and they reached the house just after nine-thirty.

Medway was in one of the rooms which had been hardly touched by the explosion, and he came forward with a smile to greet Dawlish.

'I've heard something of what's been happening,' he said. 'Congratulations, Captain Dawlish.'

'Thanks. But we haven't finished yet,' said Dawlish hurriedly. 'Where are the three people who came here yesterday?'

'There's a gardener's cottage near, and they're all staying there,' said Medway. 'None of them has tried to get out.'

Dawlish snapped: 'Did anyone else visit the cottage? There were three people when I last heard.'

'A fourth man came late last night,' said Medway. 'In the early hours, around two o'clock.'

'Right,' said Dawlish, 'then we'd better get on with it.'

His opinion of Medway rose considerably when he learnt that arrangements for the raid on the cottage were already made, and awaited only the signal to move forward. Medway went with Dawlish and Beresford.

The Home Guards, joining the police, made a complete circle about the cottage. That formed, they closed in. Dawlish, Beresford, and Medway approached the front door, armed and prepared for shooting. There was utter silence until they reached the garden gate.

Then Dawlish snapped:

'Look out, Medway!'

He saw the front door open a little, and a moment later the snout of a machine-gun. The three of them flung themselves forward as the machine-gun spattered the earth with bullets. Almost as it started, Home Guards opened up with tommy-guns, and bullets crashed against the door.

Beneath the hail of fire, Dawlish crept along a hedge which separated the path from the front garden. Beresford was just behind him, and Medway followed close on their heels. From the back of the house came further shooting.

Beresford muttered: 'They expected us all right.'

'They thought that they might get away with it,' said Dawlish. 'Wait here a moment.' He rushed forward towards the cottage, reached the cover of the wall, and edged forward. In a few seconds he was poking his gun towards the opening of the door. He saw the snout of the machine-gun withdrawn, and fired on the instant.

He heard a gasp.

Ignoring the danger he crashed against the door. It swung wide open, caught the machine-gun, and sent it flying from the grasp of the shabby little man.

Beresford, Medway, and others crowded into the house. Suddenly the sound of high-pitched laughter drifted down the stairs.

It was so eerie that all of them stopped and glanced about uneasily.

The laughter continued, as if from someone insane. Dawlish moved towards the stairs, and as he went he said softly:

'The simple-minded Mrs. Benn, I wonder?'

No one answered.

Dawlish led the way to the landing. There were three doors, and all three were closed.

The laughter was coming from the nearest room.

Dawlish tried the handle, and it turned. Standing to one side he flung the door back. As it swung open he saw a little old woman with dishevelled grey hair, whose hands were raised in ecstacy.

From both of them showered a glittering stream of precious stones.

Dawlish saw that she had a string of pearls about her neck, and other jewels pinned to her dress. She drew back a little, as if suddenly afraid; and then she cackled:

'Look what I've found! Look what I've found!'

Beresford muttered: 'She's crazy.'

'It's all right, Mrs. Benn,' said Dawlish soothingly. 'We just want to look at them, that's all. May I see?'

He held out his hand.

The woman backed away, her eyes suddenly grown cunning. But as she moved, two or three of the gems fell from her hands. One struck the floor immediately in front of Dawlish, and his foot went down on it before he could draw back.

He drew it away abruptly, and stared down in astonishment. The 'jewel' had been crushed to a white powder, and in the powder was a tiny slip of paper.

Slowly, he stooped to retrieve it. There was writing on the paper in code, and at the moment indecipherable, and as he saw this, he felt a great surge of satisfaction.

Beresford's jaw dropped in wonder.

'My oath, Pat! Did you know?'

Dawlish looked at him distantly.

'Know? Of course I didn't. I just thought that there was something odd about that jewel robbery. Paste stones, with messages inside. What a communication system!'

It was a week later when Dawlish went to Audeley Street, and saw Colonel Whitehead.

There had been much to satisfy him.

Tim Jeremy was out of danger, while Felicity, Elvira, and Robbie had not suffered more than shock from the explosion. Robbie and Elvira, he knew, had been debating the wisdom of getting married during what was left of Robbie's extended leave. After the shock of realising that her uncle was in the spy-ring, Elvira had recovered well, and between her and Robbie there was a deeper understanding.

Rennett and Kohn were waiting trial, with the other prisoners.

It had been proved on the shabby man's confessions that Dawlish's summing-up of the situation had been reasonably on the mark. Under the cover of the Lex Oil Company espionage had been carried on for years. Of the directors, only the half-witted Mrs. Benn had been innocent, wherein Dawlish had been wrong. Trivett had said with a wry grin that Dawlish could not have everything his own way.

Whitehead's greeting was almost an effusive one.

'Dawlish, I congratulate you,' he said. 'I'd been told that you smelt these things out, and I'm beginning to believe it! As a result of your jewel discovery raids have been carried out on jewellers in the bazaars all over India. The whole system of exchanging messages in faked gems has been exposed. There wasn't a bazaar of any consequence which didn't have at least one agent.' He frowned suddenly, and added: 'The country is still riddled with spies, of course, but we've gone a long way towards breaking the back of the organisation.' He smiled again. 'I've had messages from the Cabinet about you,' he added. 'Warmest congratulations. You'll be sent for in the next day or two, I think.'

Dawlish smiled. 'Well, I'll get over that.'

'What a man!' chuckled Whitehead. 'Yes, you'll get over it, and then you'll come back to the office and complain that nothing ever happens!'

A few minutes afterwards Dawlish was walking quickly towards the flat and Felicity. Half-way along Jermyn Street he saw Robbie Graham hurrying towards him. Waving an exuberant hand he called out:

'I'll be back soon, Pat. Can't stop now. Vi's said "yes", I'm off to fix the licence. Cheer-ho!'

ABOUT THE AUTHOR

John Creasey, born in 1908, was a paramount English crime and science fiction writer who used myriad pseudonyms for more than six hundred novels. He founded the UK Crime Writers' Association in 1953. In 1962, his book *Gideon's Fire* received the Edgar Award for Best Novel from the Mystery Writers of America. Many of the characters featured in Creasey's titles became popular, including George Gideon of Scotland Yard, who was the basis for a subsequent television series and film. Creasey died in Salisbury, UK, in 1973.

THE PATRICK DAWLISH MYSTERIES

FROM OPEN ROAD MEDIA

Find a full list of our authors and
titles at www.openroadmedia.com

FOLLOW US
@OpenRoadMedia

EARLY BIRD BOOKS

FRESH DEALS, DELIVERED DAILY

Love to read?
Love great sales?

Get fantastic deals on bestselling ebooks delivered to your inbox every day!

Sign up today at
earlybirdbooks.com/book